Steadfast

Praise for Jennifer Johnson's Books

Tomorrow's Child
Tamara will do about anything to save her dying daughter. Then the story gets complicated. I started reading and was late to an obligation because I couldn't put it down. ~Amazon Review, 5 Stars

Faithful
"...more than a love story. This is a story about the closeness of two sisters and the sacrifices we make for those we love. If you love a happily ever after, then read this one." ~Good Reads, 5 Stars

Rescue Me
"There is chemistry between the two characters and you can feel it... If I could give this book 6 stars, I would! ~Beck's Book Picks

"With just enough passion blended with just enough lightheartedness, Jennifer Johnson has truly created a novel that I think is stellar." ~Romancing the Book Reviews, 4 Stars

Rescuing Riley
Sequel to *Rescue Me*
"...a different type of romance—a love that must endure the breathtaking challenges life throws at us and deals with the precarious tightrope walk of a true-to-life marriage."
~Good Reads Review, 5 Stars

Double Dog Dare
If you love a heartwarming story about falling in love, then I dare you—double dog dare you even, to get yourself a copy of this great book. ~Long and Short Reviews, 4 Stars

Cars, Cobras, and Concertos
"Given the unlikely pairing of a mechanic and a concert violinist, I wasn't sure what to expect.... Surprisingly, Ms. Johnson made the plot and characters believable and likable without being saccharine sweet. I can't wait to see her next offering!" ~ Amazon Review, 5 Stars

STEADFAST

Family Tangles: A New Spin on Some Ancient Tales

Jennifer Johnson

STEADFAST
Copyright © 2017, Jennifer Johnson
Trade Paperback ISBN: 978-1-946608-18-5

Editor, Karen Block
Cover Art Design by Calliope-Designs.com

Digital Release, September 2017
Trade Paperback Release, September 2017

Media > Books > Fiction > Romance Novels
Categories:

STEADFAST

They met at daybreak on a rock called Steadfast.

Widow Jane Stanford has no family other than her mother-in-law Laura. When Laura goes to her childhood home to die, Jane follows to take care of her.

Jane meets Bo Anderson, who has no idea the land he's farmed all his life belongs to Laura. In spite of the complications, Bo reaches out in kindness to make his new neighbors feel welcome. And Jane finds a kindred heart in a man who values family even more than the land. But a long-held secret threatens to break apart the budding relationship. Can the steadfast love and faithfulness of two people heal the brokenness of the past?

"Now Naomi had a relative… a man of standing, whose name was Boaz."
    Ruth 2:1

Chapter One

"I'm going back to Haven, Alabama," Laura declared.

Jane wiped her eyes. It was five in the morning, and she'd just finished a double shift at the all-night diner. Couldn't her mother-in-law wait to make life and death decisions until Jane had had some sleep?

A garbage bag lay open on the couch Jane was using as a bed. A meager pile of clothes Laura had gotten from a Goodwill store rested in the middle of the black folds. The woman acted as if she didn't have a dime to her name, though her Ph.D. and prolific research in genetics had secured her a teaching position at the University. So involved was Laura in the creative structure of DNA that she neglected the basic details of survival like eating and bathing.

Laura was dying or, at least, she thought she was. Jane didn't blame her for wanting to go to her hometown to do it. The fire that had destroyed their house had also killed Jane's husband and father-in-law. Both Laura and Jane had been widowed and homeless in the same day, but Jane had found them a one-bedroom apartment until they could get back on their feet. Laura had refused to move again, so Jane had slept on the couch ever since. She didn't mind. In her quirky way, Laura had endeared herself into Jane's heart, accepting her without reservation. Lately though, the older woman had gotten a death notion. It probably didn't help that the cemetery plot salesman had come by trying to drum up business by advising Laura she needed to get her affairs in order.

"When are we going?"

"We're not going. I'm going. This town has been your home for a long time, but it's done nothing for me. I'm not dying here. I'm going home." Laura was about to start a sabbatical, so she wouldn't be missed at the school.

"I think you're supposed to research during your time off—not go home to die."

"I am going to research. My impending death. At the place where I was born."

Jane envied the older woman's knowledge. Jane didn't know where she'd been born, since she'd been found abandoned just north of the Mexico-Texas border. She'd lived with so many foster families that her first real home had been when she married Laura's son, Mandy. He had been a good tipper at the restaurant where she worked, very quiet and very sweet. One morning as her shift was ending, he'd asked her to marry him, and she'd laughingly agreed. Then when he drove her to the courthouse, she realized he hadn't been joking.

Jane remembered studying Mandy's pale hand as it grasped her much darker one. She had shaken her head. "Your parents," she said. "They probably don't want a wetback as a daughter-in-law."

He hadn't flinched at the slur. "My mother is scientist. She believes genetic diversity creates superior human beings."

Confused, Jane shook her head.

Mandy laughed and kissed her. "My parents will love you. Trust me."

Mandy was right. His mom and dad had welcomed her wholeheartedly, enveloping her in the warmth of a family she'd never had before. The two years they had been married were the happiest of her life, and when Mandy died, she'd never considered anything but staying with Laura. Jane was the only family the woman had, and Laura was the only family Jane had known.

"Are you sure?" Jane asked.

Laura pursed her lips—an affirmation if Jane had ever seen one.

"Maybe I could take you there for a visit. I can ask for some time off work. We could stay a week. Make it into a vacation."

"I'm going today." She picked up her bag and twirled it closed. Walking over to Jane, she hugged her. "I love you, girl. You've been a good daughter."

Jane accepted the hug. "That sounds like goodbye."

"It is."

"How are you going to get to Haven? Walk? It's not even in the same time zone as us, or did you want to take the car?"

"You know I don't drive." The woman had mapped strands of DNA, but she'd never bothered with a driving test, preferring to walk or take a bus.

"So, I should drive you then?"

"You're so young. Stay here and find a boy to marry. Didn't you say Jack Brayer asked you out? You should go out with him. Start living again."

"Jack Brayer doesn't tip. At all. Then he has the gall to ask me out. I'd sooner stay single than give him anything but his burger and fries. If you want to go back to your hometown to die, I guess I could drive you, but you can wait until I can get someone to cover for me, right?"

Laura kissed her on her cheek. "I'm going to take the bus. It leaves at nine o'clock."

Jane sighed. "Please wait a few days until I can work something out."

"I've waited too long already. This town has taken everything from me. I'm done here."

"I'll drive you." Maybe Laura would get there, look around, and decide there was nothing for her there. Then Jane could bring her back. But if the woman decided she was going to stay...well...Jane would stay too. Laura may not have given birth to her, but she was the closest thing to motherly love Jane had known. Laura was family, and family meant something.

11

Jane packed her own suitcase, and they walked out to the car. Mandy had made the last payment on it ten days before the fire, so they owned it outright. She and Laura hadn't acquired too much since then. Jane had been too busy trying to take care of Laura and grieving her own husband to fool with shopping. There was something to be said about not having much. It made moving easy. Or at least closing everything up until Laura got this notion out of her head that she was dying.

****

No Trespassing.

Jane sighed as she drove slowly past the second posted sign.

What was she going to do if some xenophobic man in overalls, wearing a *We Dare Defend our Rights* emblazoned baseball hat and holding a shotgun met them out here in the middle of nowhere?

"Are you sure this is it?" she asked Laura once again.

"Yes, I'm sure. Look. There it is up ahead."

Jane continued on and peered through the car window at the tiny house ten feet from the dirt road. There was a tree growing where the front porch stairs should have been. She turned to Laura. "You're kidding, right? This is where we're staying?"

The smile beaming on the older woman's face extinguished any hope this was a joke. Laura exited the car and strode toward the building. With a sigh, Jane followed. "Isn't it beautiful? It's just like I remember."

The peeling paint on the clapboard house at some point had been white. The front windows, several panes cracked or broken, had a layer of dirt on the remaining glass, making it difficult to see inside. "Did it have stairs to get to the porch back then, or did you just climb the tree?"

"Of course, it had stairs." She walked to the edge of the porch and grasped the one remaining handrail attempting to pull herself up.

"Don't do that! You're going to break your leg." Jane hurried over to spot her and watched her climb up onto the wooden porch.

"There. See? That wasn't so hard." She stood and brushed off her pants. "Go look in the trunk and get me those bolt cutters, will you?"

"What do you need bolt cutters for?"

"So I can get in the house."

Suspicion erupted in Jane's mind. She looked at the padlock on the door. "Don't you have a key?"

Laura shot her an exasperated expression. "Well, of course I had a key at one time, but it's been lost for years. Now go get me those bolt cutters."

"Are you sure this is your house?"

"Of course, I'm sure. I spent the first eighteen years of my life here until Dad..." She shook her head. "Never mind. I'll get them myself."

"No. No." Jane pivoted and headed to the car. "I'll get them." Opening the trunk, she retrieved the cutters. Noting the box of cleaning supplies and several other tools, Jane realized Laura had planned for this. She walked back to the house but didn't attempt the tree/rotted stair climb.

"If you had some paper—some proof—that it was okay for us to be here, I'd feel a lot better about all of this." Well, not a lot better, but, at least, she wouldn't feel as if they were trespassing on someone else's property.

Laura gave her a look of exasperation and sent her a *come here* signal with her hand. "The papers burned in the fire along with everything else. Now, bring me the cutters."

Jane gripped the tree and ascended to the porch. "Did you see those no trespassing signs? They look relatively new."

"Good. Maybe no one will bother us."

"They aren't your signs, Laura." Jane held the cutters down at her side. "And this isn't your land. It can't be. You've been gone for decades."

"It was my daddy's, and when he died, it came to me." Laura reached down and took the tool from Jane's slack fingers. "You don't believe me? Go to the courthouse. In fact, that's a good idea. Why don't you make that your goal today? Get a copy of the property record, so I know how much of this land is mine."

"I wish you'd told me what we were getting into. I thought we were going to a hotel or something."

Laura grasped the doorknob and turned it. When the door didn't move, she put her shoulder against the wood and shoved once, twice, before it flew open. Laura stumbled with the force but kept a firm grip of the knob and regained her balance. "Why would I stay in a hotel? I'm from here."

Maybe because this place isn't livable.

Jane stood at the threshold and surveyed the house. It was bare. Not a stick of furniture anywhere except a cabinet with a sink and an ancient refrigerator in what Jane surmised was the kitchen. Years of dust and cobwebs blanketed everything. She studied a hole in the corner and hoped it wasn't home to a rat or…snake. Jane shivered.

"Let's go to a hotel."

"No."

"There's no furniture. Where are we supposed to sit or…or sleep? I haven't slept in thirty hours."

Laura wrinkled her nose. "Child, go on to a hotel. There's one in Haven."

"Come with me."

She shook her head.

Jane raised her hands in frustration. "We can't live here. Even if there was furniture, we have no dishes, no pots and pans to cook with. Is there even a stove? What about electricity and running water?"

"We'll get all that stuff."

"When? It's lunchtime, and I'm hungry. You expect us to set up a house in one afternoon?"

"I'm staying here."

The stubborn set of the woman's lips elicited a sigh of resignation from Jane. There was no arguing with her sometimes. "Then I'm staying with you."

God help me. Whether it was a prayer of appeal or a declaration of stupidity, she didn't know.

She was too tired to figure it out at this point. She had to get Laura back in the car. At least then, Jane could drive them into town for better accommodations. Sleeping on the floor in a place where wild animals had been seeking shelter for the last several years was a bad idea.

Her stomach growled. "Can we at least go get something to eat?"

Laura's smile fell a bit. Her gaze strayed to Jane's midriff. Obviously, she'd heard the stomach growl too.

Jane knew the look. *Aw gee, do we have to?*

"Can't you just bring some food back here?" Laura hedged.

"No. We'll go into town, find a restaurant, eat, then make plans for what we'll need to stay out here." Jane purposely didn't agree to drive back out here tonight. If she could just get her in the car....

Laura sighed, and Jane bit back a smile knowing she'd won the battle.

"I suppose we could grab a bite to eat, and I only packed the one sleeping bag."

"What was I going to sleep on?"

Laura shrugged. "This is my homecoming. Not yours. You were supposed to stay in Linten City and go on a date with Jack Brayer."

"Where you go, I will go. Where you stay, I will stay. Your people will be my people...."

"Yeah. Yeah." Laura waved a hand in dismissal. "And your God will be my God. It'd be nice if you could come up with something original."

"It's my way of telling you that you aren't getting rid of me."

Shaking her head, Laura walked out on the porch and climbed down with the aid of the tree and rail. Jane followed.

"Shut the door," the older woman ordered.

"What for? Are you afraid critters will get inside? Too late for that."

****

Bo walked into the small room where his mother lay on the stretcher in the emergency department. He'd been called out of the field by Amber Fellows, owner of *The Bread Basket* and his partner in the produce market part of the business.

"Bo," she'd said. "Your mama is okay, but she's on her way to Haven Hospital because she nearly choked to death on one of your free-range chickens."

When MayLynn saw him walk into the room, fear flashed in her eyes. But when she blinked, it was gone.

He stood next to the bed. "What happened?"

"I'm fine." She shifted on the bed. "Will you take me home?"

"Amber said you almost died."

His mother glared at him.

Sally Lawson, the ER nurse, stepped into the room. "Hi, Bo. Mrs. Anderson. Good news. You don't have any broken ribs."

Bo shook his head incredulously. "Broken ribs? I thought she choked on some food."

"She did, but some woman performed the Heimlich maneuver on her." Sally walked over to the computer monitor on a cart next to the bed. "She has some bruising, but it's a small price to pay for being alive."

Bo turned to her. "Who did the Heimlich on you?"

"I don't know."

Bo studied his mother's face. The way she had snapped at him implied maybe she was embarrassed about the whole episode. He couldn't say he blamed her. Still. Someone had saved her life today. He'd talk to Amber later and find out who the good Samaritan was so he could express his gratitude.

"Is Mom okay?" Bo asked Sally. "Is she going to be admitted?"

Sally shook her head. "Blood pressure is a little elevated, but that's not surprising. Doctor says she can go home, but she should rest and watch for any issues with breathing. Sometimes a person will aspirate a piece of food and it can cause problems."

"I can breathe just fine." MayLynn shouted then clutched her throat and coughed.

He raised his eyebrows at Sally. "No. She needs to—"

Sally put up a silencing hand and waited until MayLynn's coughing fit had subsided.

MayLynn glared at them both. "Don't…say…anything else. Just take me…home, Bo."

"She can breathe just fine, and we shouldn't say anything else. At least, that's what she said in between the coughing." Bo made the pronouncement but had serious doubts. He hoped Sally would disagree.

Sally pursed her lips and watched her patient for another minute. "All rightie. Come back in if she decides she can't breathe just fine."

Chapter Two

Geez, it's hot down here.

Even though the sun was just peeking over the horizon, Jane felt the humidity clinging to her like an uncomfortable blanket. She'd gone to the courthouse yesterday hoping to resolve the issue of Laura's idea that she owned the land. In Jane's mind, there's no way Laura could have kept up the taxes for as long as she'd been gone. When? Since she was eighteen? That had been thirty-five years ago. Laura couldn't even keep a plant alive in the house because she forgot to water it. Maybe if Jane found out the land belonged to someone else, Laura would be willing to abandon this crazy notion she had of living here. They could go back home to Linten City where the heat didn't make it so hard to breathe.

But when Jane had located the county records, she nearly fell off the stool in the workroom. Not only did Laura own the house, but she owned one thousand acres surrounding it. Jane had come back with her head fuzzy with the implications of it. If Laura owned all of this land, then why was somebody else farming it?

Jane asked Laura about any agreement she had with the Anderson family, who apparently were farming the land, about rental—or what? A portion of the profit from the crops maybe, but the woman, in typical Laura fashion, had waved her hand dismissively. "You know I'm no good with plants."

"I'm not asking you about farming the land. I'm asking if these people have an agreement with you to use your land to plant their crops."

"I was a teenager when I left here. I don't know what kind of deal my father made."

"Who's been paying the taxes all this time?"

"Well, I did do that. Daddy made me swear on his soul I'd do it every day on my birthday, so I did."

In exasperation, Jane had thrown up her hands. "You forget when your birthday is half the time."

"And you always remind me."

With the conversation still fresh in her mind, Jane had risen early and set out to walk Laura's land. A thousand acres was too big for her to measure on foot, but the boundaries were not straight lines. According to the deed, there was a hill to the east of the house and a large rock at the top called Hesed, which looked within walking distance. Imagine that. A rock with a name.

Jutting into Laura's land, the rock marked the property owned by Zachary Anderson. Perhaps it was divided that way because it wasn't good farmland. But someone was making use of the land. Today Jane would need to meet them and find out what was going on.

The beginnings of dawn was enough light to illuminate the field. Beyond it, a copse of trees rose up like an oasis in a desert of flat land. As she approached, a chorus of insects grew. What were they? There must be thousands, as loud as the sound was.

Instead of going through the trees, she arced around them and gasped. There was the hill, and above it, the rock and a barn. The barn had a flat roof with a wooden staircase attached to the front that spanned over two large doors on the ground level. The stairs led to a wooden balcony and a door on the upper corner. Whose barn was it? Had Laura's family built it or had the Andersons? It certainly was in better shape than Laura's house.

Jane followed a dirt road that led up to the structure. She scaled the hill and stood looking at the pale rock with dark veins running through it. Massive, the boulder stood about waist high and was easily fifteen feet across. She reached forward and touched its smooth surface. What kind of stone was it?

Jane hoisted herself up on the rock and scooted across

it. She lay back, kicked off her shoes, and looked skyward.

Incredible.

Low pink clouds wisped above the fluorescent crescent sun in the ever-lightened canvas, and the thousands of stars, so bright the night before, had disappeared. Jane stared at those stars for at least an hour, amazed at the glitter-encrusted nighttime quilt. She'd never seen so many stars, and it reminded her of a story from the Bible. God had told Abraham, 'Count the stars, if indeed you can count them. So shall your offspring be.'

Jane had hoped one day she and Mandy would have children, but they never had gotten around to it. She thought they'd have so much more time than they'd had—time to have kids and raise them and grow old together. But none of it was meant to be, apparently.

A flash of light ran across the rock, and Jane turned toward it and startled. A truck had arced in front of the barn and was backing up to the entrance. Seeing it, Jane realized she could hear the engine blending with the song of the insects. A man exited the truck. He walked to the barn and, in a moment, swung open one of the wide doors. He released the tailgate of the truck and reached into the bed and retrieved a large bag. Hefting it on his shoulder, he carried it in the barn. By the size of the bag and his movement, Jane surmised the bag likely weighed a hundred or more pounds. In a moment, he returned and carried another bag into the building.

Jane sat up to get a better look at him. He wore jeans and a white T-shirt with some logo emblazoned across the back. His hair was cut short, and when he stepped into the ray from the light inside the barn, it looked the color of rust, similar to Mandy's hair. Who was he? A worker from the Anderson farm, perhaps? She was sure he'd spot her if he looked in her direction, but she didn't leave the rock.

She watched his progress. Four bags now. Coming out, he swung the door shut and locked it. Then he went to the cab of the truck and retrieved something from inside. The man walked toward the building again, this time going up the staircase. He paused at the door and was in the process of unlocking it, when he stopped, his head turned toward her.

He's spotted me.

He took a few steps back and placed a hand on the railing. "*Buenos dias. ¿Cómo estás?*"

He thinks I'm Latina. Well, I am, even if I don't speak a word of Spanish.

"You're standing on a balcony, and it's just past daybreak. Somehow I expected you to say something more inspiring."

He leaned forward as if to get a better look. "I apologize. You speak English. I thought you might be a migrant worker."

Jane let his comment pass. "I think your line is supposed to be, 'Romeo, Romeo, wherefore art thou, Romeo?'"

"Not only do you speak English, but you quote English playwrights. What are you doing here in the middle of my soybean fields?"

"Your soybean fields? This land is yours?"

"Yes."

No hesitation whatsoever. He must be Zachary Anderson. Did he not know that at least half of the land they could see didn't belong to him or was he just a really good liar? From here, it was difficult to see the expression on his face. "How interesting."

"You know what I find interesting? A woman sitting on a rock on my land quoting Shakespeare to me."

Oh, he was smooth, all right. Well, Jane could be smooth right back. "Hark, what light through yonder window breaks? It is the east, and Juliet is the sun."

He rested his elbows on the railing. "But soft."

"What?"

"It isn't 'hark.' It's 'But soft! What light through yonder window breaks? It is the east, and Juliet is the sun.'" He turned his face to the lightening sky. "Arise, fair sun, and kill the envious moon, who is already sick and pale with grief, that thou, her maid, art far more fair than she."

Jane's mouth fell open in shock. *Wow.* Shaking off her surprise, she replied, "I'm impressed. A farmer who knows his Bard."

He straightened. "Thank my tenth grade English teacher, Mrs. Armstrong, for the assignment. I got an A for reciting the soliloquy in front of the class and a date with Emily Jackson who fancied herself a Juliet to my Romeo. Are you alone?"

"If I were, would I tell you?" Jane straightened her legs, stretching them out on the rock top and crossed her ankles.

"I'd rather know if a couple of guys are going to charge up here and kill me while you're distracting me with clever dialogue and your bare feet."

Jane's gaze flickered to her toes. Was he flirting with her? More importantly, was she flirting with him? She didn't dwell on it. And she certainly didn't want to reveal too much to Zachary Anderson this morning. Not until she knew the best way to handle this delicate situation of what was likely going to be a property dispute.

"If we were going to kill you, we would have done it while you were unloading bags and putting them in the barn. You get an F from me for observation. I've been sitting here the whole time."

He didn't speak for a moment, then said, "I was about to brew some coffee. Why don't I fix you a cup and bring it down to you, and you can tell me why you're trespassing at just past five in the morning."

"Coffee sounds good." Really good. She'd slept in the car last night because Laura wouldn't agree to stay in a hotel and the furniture rental place couldn't deliver until today. Jane refused to sleep on the floor in the house until she knew for sure she wouldn't wake up nose to nose with a rat or a raccoon.

Cotton candy pink and blue painted the sky now. If they were home, she'd be at the diner getting ready for the breakfast crowd. Hard to believe every morning of her life she had missed this gorgeous scenery.

Squeaky hinges sounded above her, and the door closed. Then Zachary's heavy-booted feet on the wooden balcony and down the stairs. Jane moved to the edge of the rock and hung her feet down over the side. Zachary was walking across the expanse of shorn grass between the barn and the rock with a ceramic cup in each hand. When Jane raised her gaze to his face, their eyes met and something inside of her chest hitched.

She should have left while he was making the coffee. This early morning visit could make an awkward situation even more so. She didn't want to tell him who she was or why she was here. That conversation needed to happen with Laura.

He stopped next to the rock and held the cups of coffee out to her. The aroma wafted in the air, and her mouth began to water. She took the cups, and he turned his back to her and hoisted himself up beside her. He held out a hand, and she placed one of the mugs in it.

"I'm Bo," he said.

"Is that a nickname? I thought Zachary Anderson owned this land." At least part of it, but she wasn't going to bring that up.

"Are you going to tell me who you are and why you're sitting on my rock next to my barn in my soybean field?"

He'd had enough of the pleasantries and small talk. Jane sipped the coffee. Oh, it was good, and worth a little information at least.

"My name is Jane, and I'm...staying close by. I read about a rock named Hesed, so I wanted to see if I could find it. This is it, isn't it?" She patted the surface of the rock, and in the quiet, the slapping sound appeared loud.

He studied her a moment. "Where did you read about Hesed?"

"The courthouse. Property records." Jane hoped he didn't ask why she had been looking at property records. If he knew he'd been using land that didn't belong to him, then even that little bit of information could make him nervous. Not a bad thing necessarily. "The surveyor described a hill and a large rock called *Hesed*. Did you know this rock had a name?"

Bo sighed, as if he were recalling a happy memory. "Yeah."

Jane waited for him to say more, but he didn't. "Hesed. I've never heard that word before. Do you know what it means?"

He set his cup next to him and leaned back on his hands. "It's a Hebrew word for steadfast or loving kindness. You'd think a field that has a boulder in it would have rocky soil, but it doesn't. The soil is loamy, really good for beans or any crops, really. Hesed is the only rock anywhere around. I used to come here as a kid and make up stories about how it got here."

Janie didn't respond right away. It was strange a rock this large would be here when the dirt around it wasn't rocky at all.

"How did Hesed get here?"

He shrugged. "Who knows?"

He had dismissed the mystery years ago, obviously. The rock simply was, and how or why it was here didn't matter to him anymore. But it used to matter to him. "You do, don't you? Or, at least the little-boy-you who made up the stories knows how the rock got here."

His lips slowly turned up in a smile. "I suppose I could tell the most believable one."

"All right. I love a good story."

He cut his eyes to her, making Jane think this really was going to be a good story.

"A long time ago there lived a giant. He was a miner, and he found gold in the foothills of the Appalachians in north Alabama. He grabbed a handful of rock and tore it out of the earth, and he made a cave. He put most of the gold in the cave for safekeeping. But a few pieces of gold he kept, and he threw them as far as he could. They landed here, and he put the piece of the rock he had torn out to make the cave here as a marker, so when he's ready to claim his gold, he'll pick up Hesed, and he'll go back to north Alabama and fit it in like a puzzle piece. Then he'll know where his gold is."

"How much time did you spend digging under Hesed looking for the gold he threw?"

He chuckled. "Most of one summer till my dad put me to work in the fields. He said if I wanted to dig in the dirt, I might as well make it productive. It's been a long time since I thought of that giant or his gold. What about you? How do you think the rock got here?"

Jane sipped her coffee. "I think it had something to do with two families feuding."

"The Montagues and Capulets?"

"No. I was thinking more like the Hatfields and McCoys. The families hated one another, so they would meet at this hill every Saturday and shoot at each other. One day Gladys Hatfield was looking over her gun barrel and spotted Lancelot McCoy aiming his gun at her. He had the prettiest blue eyes she'd ever seen. He closed one of those pretty blue eyes and pulled the trigger and shot a snake that had been hanging in the tree above her. She fell in love with Lancelot right then. So, after she ate some snake stew, she snuck over to the McCoy homestead that night and kidnapped him, which was fine with Lancelot because Gladys had brought him some stew, and he realized she was a really good cook. So, they eloped to Niagara Falls, and they bought this really big rock at the gift shop as a souvenir and had it delivered to the hill on Sunday when all of their kin was in church. And when the following Saturday rolled around, everybody saw the rock with Gladys and Lancelot sitting on it side-by-side. And Lancelot said, 'Now folks, we're neighbors, and the Lord said neighbors is s'posed to love each other as theyselves, so we's gonna stop fightin' and start lovin' 'cause that's what the Lord said neighbors should do.' So, everybody put down their guns, and they stopped killing each other and started loving each other as theyselves. And they named the rock *He said* because when Lancelot told them how it was going to be, they did what *Hesed* to do."

Bo groaned. "Jane, that's about the best and corniest story I've ever heard."

Jane raised her cup and tapped the side of his. "Here's to loving neighbors as theyselves."

Bo chuckled and clicked her cup with his own. "'Cause that's what Hesed to do."

They both drank from their cups, making the toast complete.

"That's great. So, where are you staying?"

"Close by."

"Yeah, you said that. There isn't any place close by. Are you doing research for a school project?"

"Thank you for thinking I'm young enough to be in school."

"So, why would you be looking at property records at the courthouse? Don't tell me you're a lawyer."

"No. I'm a waitress. Well, I was a waitress. I had to take a leave of absence to take care of some family issues."

"So, you're in Haven because of those family issues?"

"Yes, and I probably need to get back now." Jane drank the last of the coffee and handed Bo the mug. "Thank you for the coffee." She picked up a sneaker and leaned over to put it on her foot and quickly did the same with the other one.

"I don't mind you being here, but I don't think it's a good idea to be out by yourself. This is a pretty remote area. Want me to drive you back to your car?"

Jane hopped down from the rock and bent down to readjust her foot in her shoe. "Thanks, no. It's not too far, and I like the walk."

Bo slid from the rock and stood next to her. "I hope you won't take this the wrong way, but you by yourself out here makes me worry."

"I won't take it the wrong way, and I'll be careful." Jane began to walk away from him and hoped he wouldn't press her to give her a ride. "I'll see you around. Okay?"

"Nice meeting you, Jane." His voice followed her as

she walked away.

Jane didn't look back.

****

Bo watched Jane walk down the dirt road for a few minutes then took their coffee cups upstairs to the apartment and washed them. He used the apartment as a convenience at harvest time or when he wanted to be by himself away from the well-meaning influence of his mother. When he was younger, he'd actually lived in the apartment for a few years, but when his dad died, Mom had been bereft in the big house by herself, so he'd moved back temporarily. That had been four years ago.

His thoughts returned to the woman he'd met this morning.

She looked Mexican, but she had no trace of any foreign accent. She was pretty, her black hair falling in waves over her shoulders and down her back. Her dark eyes had a sadness to them that didn't quite fit with the silly story she'd made up about Hesed. Where had she come from, and where was she staying?

Her answers had been evasive, so he figured she was hiding something, but she obviously knew something about him—or his land, at least. She knew his dad's name. Still, if she'd been doing research on Hesed, Dad's name was on the property deed. Bo didn't realize the rock's name was also on the property deed. Bo didn't even know it was part of the property description.

He placed the mugs in the drying rack on the counter and wiped his hands on a tea towel hanging on a hook on the wall. Locking up, he went downstairs and gathered some vegetables he'd picked the day before to take into town. He placed the baskets in the bed of his truck and entered the cab, cranking the engine even as he settled on the seat. Maybe he'd see Jane on the side of the road. If he did, he'd insist she get in so he could take her wherever she wanted to go. Then he could find out more about her—maybe even take her to breakfast.

But he didn't see her on the way into town, which

made him even more curious. If she'd driven from town and parked her car to walk to the barn, he should have seen it on the way there. But he hadn't seen anything. No car and no Jane.

Within twenty minutes, Bo unloaded a peck of early corn into *The Bread Basket* and displayed it in the small grocery in the corner of the restaurant. Then he sat down at the counter in front of Amber, his business partner and girlfriend. Though the restaurant wouldn't open for another half hour, Bo knew she wouldn't mind the company.

Amber wiped a floured hand across her brow. "How's your mama?"

"I checked on her before I left the house. She seems okay."

"Hey. I just made a batch of pecan rolls. Want one?"

She didn't really have to tell him. The sweet smell had enveloped him in the parking lot. It had made the drive into town worth it. "Sure."

She pulled one off the cooling rack and set it on a plate. "Coffee?"

He nodded, and she poured him a cup. "I didn't expect to see you until after lunch."

"What happened yesterday? Mom won't tell me anything."

Amber put the carafe back on the warmer and picked up her rolling pin. She flattened the biscuit dough she'd been working on. "Your mom was eating lunch here like she always does on a Tuesday. A couple of ladies came in, and the next thing I know, MayLynn's turning blue and she starts to slip to the floor. The dark-haired woman grabs her from behind, then she, sort of, heaves her forward a couple of times, and this chunk of meat flies across the room. She tells me to call 911, and then she sits MayLynn in a chair until the ambulance gets here."

"Dark-haired woman? Did you catch her name?"

"No. I've never seen either one of them before."

"Out-of-towners?"

Amber shrugged. "I'd say yes. The younger one looked

Hispanic."

"Hispanic?" An image of Jane filled his mind. It had to be her. Too much of a coincidence for it not to be.

Amber was still speaking, but Bo hadn't been paying attention. "I'm sorry. What?"

"I said Pete Jessup was in here. He knew the older woman. Called her Laura Justice, I think."

"Laura Justice?" Bo searched his memory. "I don't recall any Justices around here."

"He said her mama was a Voyles."

He tapped his finger on the counter. Could she be family? "There are some Voyles on my mom's side," he said.

"Huh." Amber picked up a glass and rubbed the lip in a small pile of flour then pressed the cup in the flattened dough.

"Did Mom act like she knew her?"

"I don't know." Picking up the dough circles, she placed them on a cookie sheet on the counter. "She started choking pretty soon after they walked in, so she didn't speak to her at all."

"And the women were definitely together?"

"Oh, yes. Sat together in the booth over there. Even wiped down the table and stacked the plates before they left, with a nice tip, I might add."

Hmm. It sounded like something a waitress would do.

"Well, if you see them, will you let me know? I'd like to thank the woman who saved Mom's life."

And find out if that woman was the same one he'd shared coffee with an hour ago.

Chapter Three

Jane heard the rumbling of the truck before she saw it. Yesterday she had gone against her better judgment and accompanied Laura to the rent-to-own place to get furniture for the house. They still had no electricity, but at least there was water in the house. After several disgusting moments of letting the water run into the pockmarked sink in the kitchen, it seemed to be mostly clear. But she didn't trust it. It tasted funny, or maybe since Jane had lived in the city her whole life, she'd never drunk water that came straight out of the ground and not from a municipal city supply.

I hope I don't get sick from drinking tainted water.

With too much enthusiasm, Laura had bought a camp stove and a dorm-sized refrigerator from a super store in Athens. She'd loaded up the back of the car with pantry supplies and kitchen necessities, after Jane adamantly refused to let her put Vienna sausages and Beanie Weenies in the shopping cart.

Honestly. A girl had her standards after all. And just because Laura was having a midlife crisis didn't mean they both had to die from eating pork intestines mixed with enough sodium to pickle a small town.

She swiped a lock of hair that had escaped from her bandana and scrubbed a stubborn stain on the corner of the kitchen floor. She and Laura had had a huge argument in the *Rent-A-Center* because Laura had only wanted to get a bed and a couch.

"What about a table and chairs?"

"What do we need those for?" Laura shook her head in derision. "We can eat on the couch."

"We will eat at the table like a family should," Jane insisted.

"There's just two of us. That doesn't constitute a family dinner."

The words hurt as if Laura had just gutted her with a dull knife. But Jane hadn't let it show. She folded her arms across her chest. *Fine. I can be stubborn too.* "I want a table and chairs."

The salesman cleared his throat. "We don't really have any dinette sets, but we got a patio set. It's got six chairs though."

Jane raised her chin and met her mother-in-law's gaze. "We'll take it."

Laura smiled "If you get table and chairs, I'm getting a flat screen television."

"The house doesn't even have electricity, and a TV will not run on kerosene," Jane snapped. That little dig had been because of the six kerosene oil lamps presently residing in their trunk.

"We'll get as much use out of the table as we do the television."

Jane turned to the salesman. "Forget the couch. We'll take the table and chairs and the beds only."

"I want the couch."

"And I want the table and chairs. But we do not have use of the television until we can get electricity. Let's wait until we get power before we rent a flat screen."

Laura rolled her eyes. "Let's get it now and save us a trip later. And I'll agree to the table as long as you don't expect me to sit at it."

Another argument for another time, because whether Laura admitted it or not, they were a family and families sat at a table to eat.

A couple hours later, their family furniture was still on the truck outside while Laura worked on installing the front stairs. They'd found a set for use with a mobile home, but it didn't quite work because of the inconveniently-placed tree. Laura had the job of solving the problem since she insisted on not cutting it down.

Raised voices drew Jane's attention. *What was going on?*

Jane looked out the window and saw the rental truck and a police car parked next to it. Two rental guys stood next to the headboard of one of the beds, watching as Laura and a man in uniform stood toe-to-toe in an obvious confrontation.

Oh, boy.

Jane hurried through the house and out the door. She grabbed the tree and swung over the edge of the porch to the ground but tripped over Laura's hammer. She sprawled face down in the dirt, blowing Alabama red dirt out of her mouth. Jumping up, she ran to Laura who was in the middle of a threat.

"This is my property, and I'll beat you over the head with this if you don't get off right now." Laura waved a stick menacingly.

"This ain't your property. Everything you see belongs to the Anderson family and has for as long as I've been on the force."

Well, that couldn't have been long. He may have the uniform on, but the policeman looked like he still ought to be in high school.

"Get off!"

The officer reached down toward his gun.

No!

"Excuse me! Excuse me!" Jane skidded to a halt in between them, her hands raised in a placating gesture toward the man. She stepped directly in front of Laura. "Please. Let me help. I'm Jane Stanford. I'm Laura's daughter-in-law."

"Step out of the way, Mrs. Stanford. I'm arresting your mother-in-law for threatening an officer of the law." He removed his handcuffs from his belt and took a step.

"If you arrest me—"

Jane shushed Laura and reached behind her to take the stick out of the woman's hand. Laura let go and Jane dropped it out of the woman's reach. "Please, sir. Laura doesn't mean any harm. This is her childhood home, and I'm sure this is just a big misunderstanding."

The man's eyes narrowed. "Her childhood home. You grew up here?"

"Yes, and I'd—"

Jane raised a silencing hand to her. Her tone was still combative, and Jane didn't want to have to bail her out of jail.

"She did, and she's been gone a long time. I promise I will sort this out with the Andersons. Have they filed a complaint against us?"

"Well." The man scratched his head. "Naw. But this is Anderson land. All of it is. Everybody knows that." Concern flitted across his face. "Are you all right?"

"Of course. We'll sort this out. Laura's sorry if she offended you, officer. I'm sure you can understand how upsetting it would be to hear that the house she grew up in doesn't belong to her anymore."

"It is still mine. It is." Laura's voice had lost its defensiveness though confidence rang in her tone. There was no space in her worldview for doubt.

Jane nodded over her shoulder to Laura. "All right, but we need to be sure."

"Jane, you're bleeding. Your nose."

Jane touched her nostril and felt moisture. She drew back her finger, saw the blood, and placed her finger back to her nose to stop the flow.

"What happened, ma'am?" The officer's eyes flicked to Laura, as if he thought she with her stick waving could be responsible. His hand moved to the holster at his belt.

****

Bo went to bed by nine, sometimes eight if the work was done. He was in a good REM sleep when a knock on his bedroom door awakened him.

Since MayLynn was the only other person in the house, he figured she was the one rousing him and that she had a good reason to do it.

"Bo, honey, I'm sorry to disturb you, but Sheriff Smith is here. He says he's got some business with you, that obviously he doesn't trust me with."

Bo sat up and swung his legs over to the side of the bed, trying to make sense of what his mom was saying.

"Should I tell him to come back tomorrow?"

He shook his head and stood, grabbing a pair of blue jeans from his dresser drawer. "I'll be right down."

"What do you think it's about?"

"I don't know, Mama."

"I hope it's not…." She sighed.

Bo turned and looked at her. She wiped her brow with a shaky hand.

"Mama, are you okay? Do we need to go back to the hospital?"

"I'm fine. I just…." Another sigh.

Bo shook his head and walked into the bathroom to slip on the pants. Whatever was going on with her and the sheriff meant he needed to get dressed. If he had to take her to the ER, he'd do it. Hopefully, whatever brought the sheriff out would be an issue easily resolved. When he stepped back into his bedroom, she was gone. He pulled a shirt from his closet and shrugged into it not bothering to button it before he jogged down the stairs.

He headed into the parlor, the room where he was sure his mother would take Caden. Company was company after all, even if it was official police business.

Bo walked into the room and saw the sheriff standing next to the fireplace in his uniform, his hat in his hand. Striding across the room, Bo offered his hand in greeting.

"Sheriff." They shook hands.

"Caden, let me get you some ice tea."

"Oh no, ma'am. I won't be staying long."

MayLynn huffed. "You can at least stay long enough to drink some tea."

Caden opened his mouth, but Bo shook his head at him. If the woman was in the kitchen fixing beverages, then he could talk to the sheriff without her commentary. He loved his mother, but she lived by the adage that she knew best and also by the truth of *If Mama ain't happy, ain't nobody happy.*

"Okay, then. Thank you, Mrs. Anderson." MayLynn nodded and walked out of the room.

"What brings you out here this evening? Not bad news, I hope."

"How do, Bo. Well, it could be. Could be. You been out to your back acreage lately?"

Bo scratched his chin, the rasp of his whiskers scraping against his nails.

"Which back acreage?"

"Where that abandoned house is."

"There's not a…" Bo began, but then he remembered there was an old house out there. "Not since…uh…Monday, I think. Why?"

"Seems there was a little problem out there with my deputy and some people who claim they own the house."

"What?"

"A-yep. Had a van out there moving in rental furniture." Caden shifted on his feet, eyeing Bo for his reaction.

Bo shook his head. *Squatters.* That's all he needed right now.

"What y'all do? Run them off?"

"Nope. Chuck was gonna bring the old lady in. Apparently, she threatened him, but the other one ran interference."

"The other one?"

"Yes. Young woman."

Gears whirred in Bo's head. "Did he say what she looked like? The young woman?"

"No. Said the old one acted crazy, and the young one looked like she'd been beat up. Made all nice. Said she'd talk to you and sort it out. I say if they haven't come to you yet, you might want to go out there and talk to them."

Bo shook his head and sighed. That house was less than a mile from Hesed. The young woman had to be Jane. His concern he'd spoken aloud to her ricocheted in his mind.

I hope you won't take this the wrong way, but you by yourself out here makes me worry.

I won't take it the wrong way, and I'll be careful.

Who had hurt her? A stranger or someone living with her in that shack?

"Or, I can just go out there right now. Escort them out of town if need be."

"Not now. Let them sleep there tonight. Honestly, I don't mind having someone out that way, but I don't want any trouble."

"Well, that is a dead-end road. A person would have to be really looking to find it. Maybe looking to be lost."

"I'll talk to them in the daylight."

"I wouldn't suggest you go out there by yourself."

"Let me think on it, huh? If you go with me, it might send the wrong impression."

"She was about to beat my deputy with a stick."

"I'll go into town in the morning and get some of Amber's cinnamon pecan rolls as a peace offering."

"You're a good man, Bo."

"He sure is." MayLynn came in carrying a tray with three glasses of tea. "Here you go, Caden."

The sheriff smiled his appreciation and took the glass. Bringing it to his lips, he drank the entire contents and set the glass back on the tray.

"Much obliged, Mrs. Anderson. Good night." He tipped his hat and strode to the door. "Be seeing you."

MayLynn placed the tray on a low table and turned to her son. "What was that about?"

"Some folks down on their luck, I think."

"What's that have to do with you?"

"They were on our property."

She laid her hand against her chest. "Who? Who is it? Where are they?"

"Mama, what is going on with you? Do I need to take you to the hospital?"

MayLynn blinked back the tears that collected in her eyes.

"That's it. We're going."

"No! Where are the people? Where on our property?"

Her panicked expression stopped Bo short. "It's fine. Nowhere close to here. I'm going to take care of it tomorrow."

She shook her head. "Oh, no. Oh, no."

Bo hugged his mother and kissed the top of her gray head. "You worry too much. Trust me to take care of it. Okay?"

****

Bo had gone back out to the barn by Hesed in case Jane showed up again, but she hadn't. He tamped down the disappointment and concern that wrestled in his gut. He remembered her face, her smooth skin, and big expressive eyes as she talked. Had she been attacked on her way back to that rundown shack? Or had she been hit because her husband had missed her? The sheriff hadn't said anything about a man at the house—just two women. But odds were she was married. Or had the man who had hit her been her father?

Curiosity tempted him to drive down the road to where the house was. He hadn't laid eyes on it in years, but he knew where it was. He turned to the left and drove slowly down the road. He turned his truck again and followed the road around a curve. The dingy white clapboard house lay ahead. Parked next to it was a late model car. No lights showed from the house, but how could there be? There were no power lines out this far.

A tree grew up through a partially torn-up set of stairs that led up to the front door. Another set of stairs had been positioned at the side of the tree, but there was no railing. Bo didn't like the looks of the house at all. The roof sagged, and though the windows were dark, he could see several of them had broken glass, which had been backed by cardboard. He couldn't imagine how uncomfortable it must be in the house in the heat of the day—probably close to a hundred degrees inside. It was no place for anyone to live.

And God forbid someone should get hurt because of the deplorable conditions. It would be on his conscience, not to mention he could be liable for it since the structure was on his property. Turning around at the end of the road, he drove by the house again and back to the main barn that was close to his home. He'd go out there around ten in the morning and figure out what kind of situation he was dealing with then. And if there was any trouble, he'd help Jane, give her a place to live even, if it came to that.

He was repairing a busted belt on the tractor when his cell phone rang a little after eight. Looking at the caller ID, he saw it was Emily Jackson, longtime friend and also his attorney. He answered the call.

"Hi, Bo."

"Hey. What's up?"

"I think you better get over here. Something's come up, and we need to deal with it today. This morning."

"Somebody hurt?"

"No. Nothing like that. But it's urgent. Can't wait."

Bo sighed. "That kind of meeting, huh? I'm legal with all the workers, Em."

"I know. Can you be here by ten?"

"Sure."

At ten on the dot, Bo sat in Emily's conference room. On the table was a large folder. Emily gazed at him with a troubled expression on her face. "I received a call this morning from Martin Steen." Steen had the biggest law office in town. "He called me as a professional courtesy before any papers were served."

"What do you mean? What kind of papers?"

"Does the name Laura Stanford mean anything to you? Laura Justice Stanford?"

Bo shrugged. "I heard she was in the diner. Pete Jessup said she grew up here, and she was a Voyles on her mother's side. Mama is a Voyles. They could be related, but Mama has never said anything to me about her."

"Laura is the daughter of Isaiah Justice who owned a thousand acres of land in this county. Isaiah died about twenty years ago, and he left all of his land to Laura."

Bo didn't know of that much acreage in the county

that wasn't his or owned by people he knew, but then again he didn't pay close attention to county lines unless it had to do with him. "Okay."

"You and your family have been farming on Laura's land for at least thirty years."

"What?"

Emily nodded. "I went to the courthouse because I didn't believe it. But it's true. Laura Justice Stanford's name is on the deed of land next to your land from Route 47 all the way out to the highway." She sat back and let that sink in for a moment, and then she stood up and opened the folder. "These are copies of her deed and yours." Emily placed the papers in front of Bo. Then she unfolded a map. "See this? I've outlined the area in question in green so you'll see. Not only are you farming her land, but the way the property line runs, she owns that right-of-way, and the barn you built may actually be on her property. It's hard to tell because the boundary isn't drawn off by longitude and latitude, but by a big rock."

Bo sighed. "Hesed."

"What? Oh, yeah. The rock has a name. Weird, huh?"

"So, what's this mean? What does she want?"

"That I can't say for sure. Martin is pushing for a settlement for all the years of use and an immediate injunction, but he could be bluffing me. I mean, we're talking about a widow woman who hasn't lived here for decades. She can't want to farm it, but maybe she needs money. We could offer to buy it for a good price and see what she says."

"Oh, man. I wasn't expecting this."

Jane's pretty face in the early morning light appeared in his mind. How did she fit in with all of this? "This Laura Stanford, does she have other family—a son, a daughter?"

"Martin didn't say."

"I want to meet her."

"No. We need to decide first what you want to—"

"I want to meet with them. Her. Today."

Emily leaned over the table, so that she was nearly

nose-to-nose to Bo. "I'm your attorney so that I can advise you. Let's come up with a plan before we meet with her."

Bo slapped the table. "She's staying in a shack that ought to be condemned. It's not safe. I want the meeting today. As soon as possible."

"Make her an offer for the land." Emily named a sum. "That's a reasonable cost for the acreage."

"No. I want to know what they need."

Emily's eyes narrowed. "Who's they?"

"Her people."

Emily straightened and crossed her arms over her chest. "Oh, come on, Bo. I didn't tell you she was a widow so you'd feel sorry for her. I told you she was a widow so you'd know there's no way she can work the land. Do not give in to this bleeding heart. She's snuck in under the dark of night, and now she's playing you."

"She could be family."

"If she were family, why didn't she come to you first before going to an attorney? And how come you haven't heard from her in all these years?"

Bo pushed the chair back and stood. "Call me when you can arrange a meeting."

"Don't do this. Listen to me."

Bo walked to the door.

"Bo, please."

He shook his head and turned back to the woman. "Em, there's more to this than property rights. Do you agree?"

Something flashed in her eyes.

"I thought so. Let's talk to Mrs. Stanford and see if she knows what it is. It's just a conversation that's probably thirty years overdue. Call me when you can arrange it." Bo grasped the door handle and pulled. He walked out the door, through the outer office, and out to his truck.

Why hadn't his dad ever told him? Why would he farm land that didn't belong to him, and how come in decades of paying taxes, Bo hadn't known any of this? How could this be? The land he'd farmed his entire life wasn't even his. My

God, that was almost a fourth of the farm. He didn't have enough money to pay her to buy it. He'd have to mortgage his land, if all the rest of it even belonged to him. Had Emily checked to see if the rest of their land really belonged to them? Bo's chest tightened at the thought, and he reached his hand up and pressed on his breastbone to ease the ache.

If his mother was true to her schedule, she would be at home weeding the flower bed. He planned on having a heart-to-heart with her to find out if she knew why he'd been working someone else's land for as long as he had been farming. And after he talked to Mama, he was going over to Eric Jenters, the CPA who did their taxes, and find out if he knew about any of this.

Surely not.

If he knew, he would have brought it up to Bo. They could have fixed it.

My God, what a mess.

In a few minutes, he pulled up to the homestead. Bo parked his truck in front of the house instead of the usual spot in the garage. He didn't have time for this. He needed to get that tractor back working, and he'd promised Amber he'd bring in some peaches and tomatoes today. He needed to do that before the lunch crowd started coming in.

Bo walked around the back of the house. MayLynn was in the flower garden sitting on her haunches pulling weeds from among her dahlias. She couldn't stand weeds in her flower beds and refused to use weed spray on them, preferring the arduous task of pulling them out by hand. With a large sunhat on, he couldn't see her face at first.

"Mama?"

The hat tipped up toward him, and his mother's sweet face appeared. "Why, Bo, what are you doing here? I didn't expect you home until at least four."

Bo often stayed in the fields through lunch, stopping in at his apartment to grab a sandwich or have an early lunch at *The Bread Basket* if he were bringing produce out there.

"Something's come up, and I need to talk to you about it."

The look of pleasant surprise that had been on her face slowly fell like sand through an hourglass. Then her hat tipped down, and she reached forward and grasped her weeding dowel and proceeded to work on a dandelion. "All right."

Bo crouched down. "Are we related to Laura Justice Stanford?"

Chapter Four

MayLynn's gloved hands stilled briefly. She reached down in the dirt, grasped the root of the plant, and pulled. "There is a woman, second cousin, named Laura Justice, yes. Her mother was my mother's cousin."

"You know she's back, right? Maybe you saw her in the diner Tuesday."

"Yes, I saw her."

"So, you know her then."

"Why are you asking me all these questions?"

"Because I just found out she owns about a fourth of our land."

MayLynn sat back and looked at him.

"Did you know that?"

She shook her head slowly.

"The land belonged to her father. Did Dad make some kind of deal with him, like a…a handshake or something to take care of the land or farm it?"

She moved a bit and leaned forward working on another weed. "I don't know."

"Do you remember her dad? His name was Isaiah Justice. They used to live here, in a little white house on the back of our land—well, what I thought was our land anyway. If they were your cousins, you knew them then."

She kept working in the dirt. The metal tool in her hand slipped, and she gouged the thick stem of a flower. She sat back and moved on her bottom to the next flower.

"Mama." Bo reached forward and removed her hat. "Are you listening to me? She owns a fourth of our land. Land Dad and I have been farming for as long as I remember. Dad never said anything to you about it?"

"What do you want me to say, Bo? I didn't know." She put one foot under her and hoisted herself up. Grabbing her tools from the ground, she strode across the garden to the edge of the patio and dropped them in the large basket where she kept them. Bo followed her.

"Do you know what kind of impact losing that much land is going to do to our business?" he said to her retreating figure.

She opened the back door and walked in the house, leaving it ajar. When Bo caught up with her, she was washing her hands in the mudroom. He laid her hat on the shelf where she kept it.

"Are you going to tell me what's going on?"

"I only know what you've told me. Some woman claims she owns some of our land."

"Some woman?"

"Yeah." She dried her hands and moved past him out of the small room into the kitchen. "So, handle it, Bo. You've been handling things very well since your daddy passed."

"Did you ever meet her? Talk to her? Did y'all play together as kids? I mean, if she grew up in that house on the back acreage that would have made her your neighbor."

"I didn't live here until your daddy and I got married. My family didn't associate with that branch of the Voyles, and she was no neighbor of mine."

Bo studied his mother who was now pulling glasses out of the cabinet and setting them on the countertop. Her sharp tone indicated she did not like Laura Justice Stanford at all. "What happened that there was a family rift?"

"That was when I was a girl. I don't know. It just was." She set the glass down with such force Bo was surprised it didn't break.

"Doesn't that seem like a big coincidence that your mom's cousin and her husband lived in a house on our land?"

She refused to look at him. "No, it doesn't. Everybody knows everybody, and it's a small world, and all of that."

"I'm going to meet her with our lawyers and see what we can work out."

"Good. Work it out. I'm sure you'll do fine. You've got a good head on your shoulders."

Bo sighed. Obviously, she wasn't going to tell him whatever she knew about the woman. "Okay. It'd be real helpful to know what I'm getting into, but since you're not willing to give me any back story, I'll just have to handle it the best that I can."

She held the glass under the ice dispenser in the door of the refrigerator then poured tea from a pitcher sitting next to the sink. "You want some tea?"

Tea? We could lose a quarter of our land, and she wants to serve me iced tea.

"No, Mama. I don't." He walked to the front of the house and let himself out.

****

Their CPA was on vacation, according to the message Bo listened to on the phone when he called him. Eric had been their CPA for close to forty years. He'd know what was going on. Bo tried his house, but no one picked up. He was just going to have to talk to him when he got back in town next week.

Bo tried to put it out of his mind as he went back to the tractor that still needed to be fixed. Jonathan, Bo's right hand man, was already elbow-deep in grease when Bo arrived. Jonathan and Bo had graduated high school together. Bo had gone off to college and come back with a degree in his pocket but not much more knowledge than Jonathan had who'd stayed behind and worked the farm for Bo's daddy. If Jonathan noticed anything was wrong, he didn't say so.

Bo wiped his sleeved forearm over his sweaty brow. "Hey," he finally said to his buddy.

Jonathan was now in the tractor seat waiting on the go to crank it. "Yeah?"

"You see a woman walking around here? Dark hair. Mid-twenties."

Jonathan quirked a smile. "Unfortunately, no. She a looker?"

Bo glared at him, not liking the man's lecherous tone. "I guess so, which is why I want you to look out for her. I think she's staying in that old house not far from my barn. It's pretty isolated out there. I don't want anyone messing with her or any of her family. If any of the hands go out that way, warn them off, will you?"

"What about Amber?"

Yeah, okay. Bo and Amber were an item in town, even though their relationship had cooled into more of a friendship in the last year. The more casual contact had seemed to suit them both, though neither of them had talked about it.

Bo shrugged.

"Who's the other woman?"

"Her name is Jane. I met her the other morning when I was taking some seed out to the barn."

"What? Is she homeless? She just shows up on your property and lives in your house?"

"I'm hoping I'll get more of the story today or tomorrow. Already, lawyers have gotten involved."

"What? Why?"

"A claim on some of the acreage, but that's between me and you. I don't want this broadcast all over the county."

"Nobody'll hear it from me."

"I know. That's why I told you. And I trust you to make sure no harm comes to Jane from any of our folks."

"She's pretty, huh?"

"Yeah, and you're married, so...." Bo shrugged, indicating that Jonathan didn't have any interest in any woman other than Susan, who'd probably clobber him if she suspected he was even thinking about cheating on her.

Emily called after lunch and said she'd scheduled a meeting for eight the next morning with Laura Stanford and her lawyer. Jane wasn't mentioned. Was she involved somehow? She had to be. Amber had said she was with Laura at the diner, and it was Jane who had saved his mother's life. Not only that, but she admitted she'd been looking at property records for his land.

Bo shook his head. *What an idiot I am. I should have known something was up.* Why else would Jane look at property records except to stir up trouble? She'd played him with her charm and storytelling, and he'd fallen right into her hands.

He came home late, and MayLynn wasn't in the den. Her bedroom door was closed, and the house was eerily quiet. That night he lay in his bed and watched the ceiling fan whir. At three, he gave up on sleep and got up. He gathered up some produce to take out to *The Bread Basket* and then headed out to his barn. His headlights hit Hesed, and he turned off the truck and walked over to it. Soon he was lying back and looking at the sky this time.

What was he going to do if he lost his land? He could make a living enough for him and Mama on less land, but he couldn't support as many workers as they now had. He'd have to let some of them go, and jobs were hard to come by, especially around here. There was nothing else to do but farm.

He half-expected Jane to show up like she had the other morning. He sure had some questions for her, like why hadn't she been honest with him about the reason she was there? Why hadn't she told him about her connection to Laura Stanford? That she knew the woman owned his land? And what was her connection to Laura anyway? Was it just a coincidence they were in the diner together? Was it really her who had performed the Heimlich on his mom? Was she just here to take away his family land, make a quick buck, and then leave? What was her story? Would he ever find out? Did he really want to?

Bo may have fallen asleep, or maybe he had been so consumed with all of the uncertainties the woman on the rock had brought that he didn't realize how much time had passed. The sun rose, and Jane didn't show up.

Bo wanted her to. He wrestled between being angry with her for not being forthcoming and being intrigued by her. Had she told that silly story about Gladys and Lancelot because she knew a family feud was going to be in their future? Was she hoping by her declaration of loving neighbors as theyselves that Bo would take it as a directive?

Bo headed to the apartment above the barn, showered, and put on a nice button-down and khakis he saved for church. He needed to make a favorable impression on Laura Stanford. Maybe she was family, but she could do a lot of damage to his livelihood, and Bo couldn't let that happen.

A lot of people depended on him.

****

They sat in the attorney's office. Emily sat next to Bo at a massive, polished, cherry-wood table in a large room with framed degrees and certificates on the wall, demonstrating how smart Martin Steen was.

Bet he didn't know a soybean from a black-eyed pea.

It was ten after eight, and the meeting hadn't started yet. Bo wondered if this was one of Steen's smooth lawyer tactics to humble the enemy. Make them wait, so they'd be irritable and edgy.

Bo glanced at Emily who was studying the map of his land. It *was* his land. All of the work he'd put into it should count for something, dammit.

"Calm down," Emily said.

Bo looked at her. "What?"

"Your leg is shaking the table. I understand you're nervous, but you need to calm down before they come in here. Trust me to work this out for you, okay?"

"How can it work out? I've been working on someone else's land for decades without compensating for the use of it."

"I'm not going to let her take it away from you just because her name's on the deed. Her dad abandoned it years ago. If it weren't for your family, it would be grown up and not worth much except the timber on it."

Timber? Did Emily have any idea how much timber was worth?

"Don't bring up timber acreage."

"My point is both of you have benefitted from the work you and your family have given to this land. She's not a farmer. She teaches biology at a college. She's a widow and has been for two years. I don't think she's going to come in here and start growing soybeans and corn and competing with you. Let's just see what she has in mind, and then we'll offer to buy the land, and go from there. Okay?"

"I don't have that kind of money."

"Who does? You'll get a loan, and you'll have a mortgage, just like the rest of us."

Bo sighed.

Footsteps sounded on the wooden floor, and the pocket door slid open. Emily rose and so did Bo. Martin Steen walked in, followed by a woman in her fifties wearing blue jeans and a denim jacket. Her hair, which had probably been auburn in her youth, was lighter, nearly blonde with age. Behind her was Jane. She wore a sundress, and her black hair was pulled back in a ponytail. She didn't meet his eyes when she came in, not until after they all had sat down and Martin Steen made the introductions. Bo shook each of their hands. When he took Jane's hand in his, his thumb moved across her skin before he broke contact. She noticed it, if the hitch in her breath was any indication.

"This is Laura Justice Stanford and her daughter-in-law, Jane Stanford. Laura, Jane, this is Bo Anderson and his lawyer, Emily Jackson."

Only then did Jane's eyes meet his, and a tiny smirk rounded her mouth until she bit her lower lip and bowed her head. Bo's own words from the other morning came to him then.

I got an A for reciting the soliloquy in front of the class and a date with Emily Jackson who fancied herself a Juliet to my Romeo.

He certainly hadn't expected to be sitting across the table from her in a lawyer's office while Emily represented him in a land war. He watched Jane's gaze flitter to Emily then back to him. Was she wondering if he and Emily were still a couple?

A hundred different things to say to her skittered across his brain. *Why didn't you tell me who you were? Were you just toying with me out at the rock? Where's your husband? What do you want from me?* So many things, but instead he simply spoke her name.

"Jane." It was supposed to be a common name, but he'd never met a woman named Jane. Plain Jane, he'd heard, but she wasn't. Not at all. He liked the name—simple and sweet. Just like how she looked gazing up at him from the rock, with her hair falling around her shoulders and her eyes as dark as the sky before the sun began its ascent and her feet crossed at the ankles stretched out before her. A simple, sweet picture, but not plain and really not that simple. More like alluring. Alluring Jane. Intriguing Jane.

She was watching him, waiting for him to say something. Where did he start? With the accusation or with a question? He opened his mouth. "You saved my mother's life this week at *The Bread Basket.* That was you, wasn't it?"

Jane blinked at him and nodded slowly.

"Thank you."

"You're welcome."

"Let's all have a seat, shall we?" Martin gestured to the chairs and took his place at the head of the table.

Martin had several folders in front of him on the table. "Laura Justice Stanford is the sole owner of a thousand acres of land which you and your family have been farming for the last thirty years, Bo." Martin laid a paper in front of Emily and Bo. "This deed shows the land was sold for a hundred dollars by Zachary Anderson to Isaiah Justice."

Bo stared at the typed paper.

Ten cents an acre. Insanity.

He laid a copy of the map Bo had already seen. "This shows the property lines. Laura owns the land from here all the way out to this road, including this right of way." Martin said. "Now I don't know how in the world you got a permit to build on land that wasn't yours, Bo, but since you did, that building is also part of Laura's property."

The hell it is, Bo thought, but he kept his mouth shut. Emily's shoe pressed down on his, and he realized his leg was moving again.

"I'm prepared to file an injunction on Mrs. Stanford's property immediately until she's compensated for all use of her land these past thirty years."

"A what?" Laura asked.

"Mrs. Stanford, let me hand—"

"You are handling it, but we didn't talk about an injunction. What is it?"

"It's a court order to stop all work on your land."

"Well, why in the hell would you do that?"

"Because it's your land."

"What's that gonna do? Cause a lot of problems."

"It's only until the Andersons pay you what they owe you, as I already explained."

"You didn't explain anything about stopping the farming. That can't be good for the crops."

Martin cleared his throat. "May I speak to my clients alone, please?"

Emily nodded to Bo, and they stood up and walked through the door. Emily closed it behind them, and they stood in the foyer.

"This is interesting," Emily said. "She cares about your farm. That's a good sign. Do you know Jane?"

"We met the other day. I didn't know who she was though."

Laura's raised voice sounded through the door, then Jane's placating one.

"Martin's earning his money with her, I think. This could go better than I expected."

"I want to do what's right, but my dad would not sell that much land for ten cents an acre. I don't believe it."

"Do you think the papers are false?"

"My dad wouldn't sell a quarter of our land and not tell me."

"Were you even born at the time?" She arched an eyebrow at him. They were the same age, so she already knew the answer to her question.

"No, but I don't think he'd do it. He was a good businessman, and he was honest. Why would he sell land to someone who didn't even live here? Why would he continue to farm it as if nothing had changed? Why would he let me build that barn knowing it was on her property? He helped me design it and everything. This land has been ours for generations. None of this makes sense."

"I've looked at the deed and the bill of sale. They've been stamped by the county clerk and filed. Even if somehow Isaiah Justice lied about all of this and made it all up, the deed is on file which makes it legally binding. Not to mention she's been paying the taxes on it and you haven't. Even if the land was yours, it wouldn't be yours without you paying taxes, Bo. Your CPA should have caught that years ago."

"Yeah, and Eric is on vacation. I can't even ask him about it."

"I'm going to file a motion against his injunction. The judge won't let your farm shut down because of a thirty-year-old deal. It would cause too much harm to your business. I think Martin is just trying to scare us."

"Well, he's doing a good job of it."

"I don't think Judge Hayling will allow it. He'd be the one to approve it."

"Aren't he and Martin golfing buddies?"

"Yeah, but he's fair, and I golf too, you know."

"They let women golf on the course?"

Emily smiled. "Sure they do, ever since we elected a woman as mayor. The mayor automatically gets a seat on the country club board."

"Ouch."

"Yep. It took until the twenty-first century, but women's rights finally made it out here to the sticks."

The door opened, and Martin stepped back. "Thank you for giving us a few minutes. Please come back inside."

Emily gestured for Bo to precede her, and they entered the room. Jane and Laura were still seated. Laura scowled at her folded hands resting on the tabletop. Jane watched Bo walk in. Her pleasant smile countered Laura's tense expression. Martin shut the door, and they sat back down at the table.

"Laura does not want to file an injunction. This is against my better judgment since you have taken advantage of this situation for many years."

"My client wasn't even aware of this situation until yesterday. I hardly think he was taking advantage of it."

"He was benefitting from it, whether he knew of it or not. And anyway, one has to wonder how he hasn't been aware of not paying taxes on that much acreage."

Bo felt his hackles rise. They were talking about him as if he wasn't even here.

"Be that as it may, your client has only paid the taxes all these years. Her father, in effect, abandoned his land, and it was left to Bo's father to take care of it, which he did very well in their absence. An injunction would be harmful to the farm, and it would be a slap in the face of any good conscience agreement made years ago between these two families."

"A good conscience agreement? What makes you say that?"

"He sold him a thousand acres for ten cents an acre. Obviously, it was a deal made between two friends when Mr. Justice left."

"I don't practice law based on deals between friends. I have the facts before me. Based on those facts, Anderson Farms owes Laura Stanfield compensation for use of her land. She's agreeable to having him continue to farm, but he's going to have to start paying rent, and the buildings on her land are hers outright."

"Hey," Laura snapped. "I have a mouth on my face and a brain in my head, and so does Bo Anderson. The only building I want on my land is the house I'm living in, which I've already told you, but you aren't listening, Martin Steen."

"I'm just doing what is in your best interest, Laura."

"My house," she said.

"All right." Martin threw the pencil down against the paper in front of him. It was the only indicator that he was angry. "Laura wants to live in her house on her land."

"Of course, Mrs. Stanford," Bo said. "But the house appears to be run down. I'm not sure it's safe to live in."

"Jane and I are fixing it up," the older woman said.

"Did the house ever have electricity?"

"Yes, of course it did."

"I don't see any power lines to the house."

"There was a big storm years ago which wiped out a lot of the lines in the county. I remember because my dad was working for the electric company. We didn't see him for about two months because of all the overtime he had to work," Emily said.

"I remember that year. We lost a lot of our crops because of the hail and flooding," Bo replied.

"It may be that because no one was living there, the electric company didn't replace the lines," Emily said.

"I can call the power company and ask about getting a line out there. The roof, though—it doesn't look safe. I have an apartment in my barn at the property line. You all could stay there until you could get your house livable again."

"It's livable now," Laura said.

"If the structure isn't sound, the county can have it condemned, and you won't be able to live in it."

"They can't keep me from living in my own house. I'd like to see them try."

Bo thought back to the story Caden had told him about Laura threatening his deputy. "It would only be until some improvements can be made to the house. You and your son and daughter-in-law are welcome to stay in the apartment. It's—"

"My son was killed in the fire that also killed my husband. Jane is all the family I have. It's just the two of us."

"I'm sorry. That must have been devastating."

"It was. I want to stay in my house. However, I'm not opposed to making it safe for Jane."

"For both of us," Jane added. She shot Laura a dark look.

Laura's lawyer leaned forward. "If a building inspector comes out there and finds the structure isn't sound—"

"Then you make sure no one kicks me out of my house, Martin. I hired you because I heard you were the best lawyer around here, so do what it takes for me to live where I want to. You got it?"

Bo suppressed a snicker as Martin wrote a note to himself to do what it took to keep Laura happy and in her shack of a home.

"What about water?"

"We have it."

"I'm not sure it's safe to drink though. I've been boiling any water we've used for drinking or cleaning with," Jane admitted.

"I've been drinking it," Laura said.

"I told you that wasn't a good idea," Jane countered.

Laura shrugged, and Jane sighed.

"Is it well water? There's no reason to think it's tainted. We test the water table periodically because of the fertilizers we use just to be sure everything's okay. If you like, we can test the water in the house."

"It may be the pipes. It doesn't run clear. Ever."

Laura snorted. "That's just a little rust. Means the water has iron in it. A little iron never hurt anyone."

"You wouldn't mind if we tested it to be sure, would you, Mrs. Stanford?" Bo asked. "It might give Jane peace of mind."

The older woman studied Bo. He prepared himself for an attack. Instead, she said. "Call me Laura."

"Now, about rent," Martin said.

Emily jumped in. "My client is prepared to buy the land from you, Mrs. Stanford, with the exception of your house and a few acres surrounding it so that you can live here as long as you want."

"She doesn't want to sell it," Martin said.

"You don't really want to bother with the upkeep of a thousand acres of farmland, do you, Mrs. Stanford?"

Laura shook her head and stood up. "I'm finished here." She scooted the chair back and began to walk to the door. "Come on, Jane. I need you to drive me home."

Jane stood up as well. She bent down and picked up her purse that must have been sitting on the floor next to her chair.

Bo stood up. "Wait. Miss Laura?" He couldn't bring himself not to use the title. He'd been taught from the cradle that any woman older than him was either addressed by her last name or had a "Miss" in front of her first name.

Laura paused and looked over her shoulder at him.

"Would you two like to come over for dinner? My mother MayLynn Anderson is your second cousin, I believe. We'd love to have you up at the house."

"Really? MayLynn would like to have dinner with me?" She chuckled. "Sure. We'll have dinner with you and MayLynn." Her smile fell. "I heard your daddy passed away. Sorry to hear about that. He was a good man."

"Did you know my dad?"

"Yeah." She studied Bo for a moment, her eyes going from the top of his head to the tip of his toes. "Yeah, I did."

Chapter Five

MayLynn's eyes shot fire at Bo. "I will not have that woman in this house."

He plunged his fork into the mashed potatoes and lifted it to his mouth, and then he cut a piece of the steak and ate it as well.

"Did you hear me?" she asked.

"Yes, I heard you."

"She's not coming here, and I will be cold in my grave before I prepare a meal for her to eat at this table."

Bo took a long drink from the milk in his glass. He didn't know where his mother's antagonism was coming from, but it didn't matter. He'd invited Laura and Jane here, and they were coming whether his mom liked it or not.

"Bo!"

He looked at her but didn't pause from eating.

"She can't come. I won't have it."

"Why don't you like her?"

"Because she's white trash."

"That white trash is our relative."

"We never associated with...with them. And we were better for it. Those kinds of people just bring everyone else down to their level. Stay away from her."

Bo felt anger rising. He'd never thought of his mother as such a snob. She had always treated the employees and workers with kindness and dignity. Why, now, was she acting as if she were so much better than Laura and Jane?

"It's not going to be easy to stay away from them since they're our neighbors and own a fourth of our farm."

Her eyes widened. "What do you mean, 'they'?"

"Her daughter-in-law is with her."

"No one else?"

Bo watched her. He saw the creases of worry around her mouth. "Did you know someone else in her family?"

"Who's with her? Who?"

"Just the two of them. They have no other family according to Laura. They're both widows. You would have something in common with Laura. With Jane, too, really."

Tears gathered in her eyes. "Don't do this."

"Tell me what I'm doing."

"I don't want her here. Neither one of them." She placed her napkin on the table next to her plate.

"You told me to handle this. Well, this is how I'm handling it. They are coming here for dinner tomorrow night."

She jumped up. "Tomorrow night! No! If you bring that woman in here, I'm leaving. I don't want to see her. I don't want to be anywhere around her."

"It's your choice. You don't have to be here, but she and Jane are coming to dinner. I think you need to make nice with her since she owns a good chunk of the land I thought belonged to us. Whatever happened was a long time ago. This is a good opportunity to put it behind you, Mom."

"I have put everything behind me. She's the one who showed up here and is dredging everything back up. I don't want her in this house, Bo. If you love me, you will abide by my wishes. I am your mother, after all." She crossed her arms over her chest.

"I do love you, Mama. But I want to do what's best for our farm." He finished his meal and put his silverware on his empty plate. He picked up his dirty dishes and headed for the sink.

MayLynn followed him into the kitchen. "This isn't it!"

"Why not?"

"Why don't you just take my word for it?"

Bo didn't respond to her question.

"Bo Anderson, you have got to listen to me about this. Stay away from her."

"Until you give me a legitimate reason to, I won't. So,

get over whatever this is, and let's move on."

With a guttural cry, she threw her plate across the kitchen in the vicinity of the sink and Bo. The plate shattered against the counter, and shards of the country roses pattern and food hit Bo. MayLynn bellowed a gut-wrenching cry and ran out of the room.

Bo shook his head in shock as he stared at a shard of plate sticking out of his forearm. What in the world was wrong with that woman? Why wouldn't she tell him what the torment surrounding Laura was all about? He sighed and began to clean up the mess.

****

Jane saw Bo's truck when she took her walk to the barn the next morning. She sat on the rock as she usually did when she came out here to watch the sun rise. The light from the window in the door came on. In a few minutes, it opened and Bo walked onto the balcony.

"Good morning," she called to him.

He walked to the railing closest to her. "This feels familiar."

"Want to join me on your rock?"

He leaned his elbows on the rail and gazed down. "Is it mine?"

"Yeah. The property line ends where the rock ends." Though she couldn't see the expression on his face, she could tell his shirt was unbuttoned. It hung open as he leaned forward.

"I guess that means this barn and the coffee in it belong to Laura. Want some of her coffee?"

"I'd love some coffee," Jane said not rising to the bait.

"All right."

In a few minutes, he joined her, shirt buttoned and tucked in his blue jeans. They sat side-by-side as they had the first day they met. He hadn't shaved, and his whiskers gave him an edginess.

"Is your apartment up there?" Jane asked.

"Yeah."

"How come you built an apartment in your barn?"

"After I came back from college, living in my parents' house felt too close, so I proposed we build a storage barn out here with an apartment up top for me to live in."

"So, you live there? I didn't realize that."

"I lived there for a while before my dad died. But my mom, she took his death really hard, so I went back to the house to stay with her. I'm still there, but sometimes I come out here when I need some space."

Jane looked at him. "Like last night?"

"Yeah."

They sat for a few minutes without speaking.

"I'm sorry I didn't tell you who I was before. I wasn't sure how you'd take it, and I didn't want you to kick us off the property if I gave you a heads-up."

"I wouldn't have done that."

"I know that now."

"I wish you two would come stay in the apartment until we can get your house livable."

"She won't leave it."

"But it's so small, and I can't imagine no air conditioning in this heat and no electricity."

"The heat doesn't bother me that much. The house is shaded pretty well with all the trees around it. I do miss hot showers though."

"You could take one in the apartment."

"I'd like that."

"Any time. I'll show you where the key is."

"Very neighborly of you."

"Well, you know what they say."

"No, what?"

"Neighbors is supposed to love each other as theyselves. And since I love a hot shower, I figure my neighbor would love one too."

Jane laughed and reached over and clinked her coffee cup to his. "Your neighbor certainly would. What time would you like us to come over for supper?"

"Seven."

"Seven o'clock. Can we bring anything?"

"Nope. I've got it all taken care of."

The sky had lightened, and a few wispy clouds tinged pink lit by the promise of the sun. Bo turned to her. "Has Laura said anything to you about my mother? Or why they left here thirty years ago after buying all this land?"

"No. I didn't even know she owned any land until last week when I came home from work, and she told me she was leaving to come here." Jane refrained from telling him Laura came here because she thought she was dying.

"And you came with her."

"As she said, we're all the family we have."

"Except for she and my mom are second cousins."

"Something I didn't know until you said it yesterday."

"What would that make us then?"

Jane shook her head. "If Mandy were still alive, I think you and he would be third cousins."

"Mandy was your husband?"

"Yes."

"He and Laura's husband both died in the fire."

"Yes. Mandy got out, but he went back in after his dad, and then he must have been overcome by the smoke. It's funny. He wasn't burned at all. The firefighters pulled him out and he looked like he was sleeping. They performed CPR, but it was too late."

The crickets sang, and it filled the silence surrounding Jane's memory of a husband who died too young. They'd been planning on having a baby, and the day after the fire, she'd started her period. She hadn't cried until then. Her hand began to move to her stomach, but she anchored it to the rock. That dream had died with Mandy.

"Do you remember the last thing he said to you?"

Bo's question whisked her to the present.

"I had taken Laura to a conference in Memphis because she doesn't drive. He said..." She smiled. "Drive safe. I'll see you tomorrow night." She slid off the rock and stood. "I guess I better go. Where's your house?"

"If you go down your road and turn right, our driveway is the first one—well, really the only one—until you get to the crossroads. We have a pecan grove in our front yard. You can't miss it." Bo stood as well. He brushed off the back of his pants and began to walk to his truck.

"Great. See you then." Jane started towards the shack. She looked up at the sky, admiring the pink and blue swirl of clouds.

"Jane?"

She turned around and saw Bo standing next to a post supporting the balcony of the barn. He patted the wood. "There's a nail here." He reached his hand up above his head. "With a key on it. It works the deadbolt. Okay?"

"Thanks, Bo."

She pivoted and followed the dirt path. She was nearly to the road, when she heard his truck start up. If he was leaving, that meant no one would be in the apartment, and for the first time in a week she could get a hot shower.

No. He didn't really mean it. He was just being nice. *Right?*

She continued to walk, but her steps slowed. She could wash her hair without worrying about accidentally swallowing the water or even looking too closely at the suspicious color of the water as it flowed down the age-stained enamel of the tub.

She hurried toward the house, already making a list of the items she'd bring with her. Shampoo. Soap. A razor. She could shave her legs!

In half an hour, she was back at the barn. The key was exactly where Bo had indicated.

Sweet man.

Jane had brought a towel as well as all her own toiletries. She would be sure not to leave any trace that she'd been there so he wouldn't regret the offer. As a matter of fact, he might not even realize she had taken him up on his suggestion. She climbed the stairs and looked over the land searching for Bo's truck. All she saw were fields, the rock, and the dirt drive leading to the road. The attorney had said Laura owned the right of way. She wasn't sure if that was the road leading to the barn or the road that led to their house.

Jane opened the door to the apartment and was surprised at how nice it was. There was a large living room and kitchen combined and two bedrooms with a bathroom in between. One bedroom was obviously the one Bo used. Jane noted the bed with the comforter pulled up to cover the bed but not exactly made up. She sighed in pleasure when she saw the bathroom with a large garden tub, which called to her more than the shower in the corner did. She closed the door behind her and walked to the tub. Turning on the faucet, a smile broke out on her face when hot water poured over her fingers. Their apartment hadn't had a tub, just a shower. In fact, Jane hadn't taken a tub bath since before the fire. She reached for her bottle of shampoo, opened it, poured a dollop under the stream of water, and watched the suds form. She undressed and folded her clothes in a small neat pile over her tennis shoes and stepped into the tub. When she lowered herself into the water, she moaned in pleasure. It had been so long. So very long since she'd done anything like this.

Thank you, Bo Anderson, for your hospitality.

She leaned against the end of the tub and watched herself in the mirrored wall. Her cheeks were already rosy from the temperature, and her lips curved upward in contentment. She sat up and turned off the water before it could flow over the side of the tub. Lying back, she kept sliding down until everything was submerged but her face, then she held her breath and let the water cover her head as well. Rising from the water, she hummed appreciatively.

Baths were wonderful. She'd have to think of some way to repay Bo for letting her bathe here. She contemplated what it could be as she lathered her hair then lay back to rinse it. From somewhere she heard a thump. Her heart skittered in fear.

Oh, no. Has Bo come back?

Sitting up, she stretched her ears to catch the slightest sound. Nothing. Had it been just the building settling? Jane didn't want to take the chance. She looked at the counter where she had placed her towel. Footsteps sounded in the apartment.

Oh my gosh. Bo is here.

Should she let him know she was in the bathroom? Quickly, and as quietly as she could, she stood up and stepped out of the tub, reaching for the towel.

The door swung open and Bo walked in, looked at her and screamed, a very unmanly squeal. Jane snatched the towel and unfurled it, covering herself.

Bo's wide eyes stared at her for a second—maybe an eternity. Then he put one hand over his eyes and held the other out in a defensive gesture. He began to back out of the room, but he stumbled against her shoes and fell backward.

He instinctively grabbed for something to keep from falling, and he connected with Jane. They both went down. Bo landed on his back. Jane sprawled on top of him. She slid off quickly, kneeling beside him. His skin was ashy pale. Had he hit his head when he fell? His eyes were open, but he had a blank stare that concerned her.

"Are you all right?" Jane put her fingers at his neck to check for a pulse.

Her touch must have revived him because he recovered instantly, sitting up. "I'm sorry. I swear I didn't know you were in here," he said in a rush and jumped to his feet.

Jane peered up at him. She held the towel to her front with one hand. Sweat broke out on his face. He whimpered and reached down, grabbed her by arm and waist and hauled her to her feet. Another whimper, and with stiff straight arms, he backed her up then turned and strode from the room. The door slammed.

"I didn't mean to interrupt. I'm leaving now," he said through the door.

Before Jane could figure out an appropriate response, she heard his rapid footfalls in the apartment and another door close. Her heart thumped a staccato beat, and she took a few deep breaths.

Should she be insulted a man had seen her naked and had screamed his head off like a B-movie actress before running away? A giggle bubbled up from her throat and erupted from her mouth. Attack of the Naked Tub Woman.

Uh-oh.

Tonight the Naked Tub Woman was having dinner with the squeamish hero of their B-movie interlude.

How was Jane going to face Bo after this? And how would Bo react?

****

Oh, my Lord, forgive me. I can't quit thinking about….

Bo shook his head attempting to get the image of Jane out of his mind, but he couldn't. She had full breasts, and her nipples were dark. Darker than he thought. Not that he'd really thought about her nipples before or imagined that they'd be the color of the black crimson dahlias in the garden. He'd seen everything in that split second before she'd covered herself with the towel, but he'd gotten another eyeful of her backside in the walled mirror. Her hair was long, to her waist, and droplets of water had trailed down to her shapely ass. He couldn't close his eyes, even though he had willed his lids down, so he'd finally just clamped his hand over his face like an idiot. And then he'd tripped and fallen, pulling her down with him. And when he'd stood up, and she'd been kneeling before him, her soft brown eyes had gazed up at him, questioning. The supple skin of her bare back and shoulders glistened from the tub water, and that had nearly undone him. He'd stood her up before the caveman in him had taken over, but his hands had encountered bare skin, the softness of her hip. He'd wanted to kiss her, capture her, pick her up, and take her to his bed in the next room. An evil voice in him was yelling, *Do it!*

But Bo was no caveman.

He'd been raised better than that. He'd snatched his hands away, shut the door, and gotten the hell out of there.

And at some point he was pretty sure he'd screamed

like a little girl.

The whole episode had been humiliating.

For him, absolutely, and probably for her too. How awful to be naked and taking a bath only to have a jerk barge in and manhandle you. She must have been scared out of her mind. Bo wasn't the type of man to scare a woman or…or gawk at one. He'd only been in a strip joint one time when he'd given into peer pressure in college, and the guilt of seeing the guys treating those women as pieces of meat had sickened him. He'd left and sworn never to go back to any place like that.

Bo wanted to go to the apartment and check on her, to be sure she was okay. To apologize to her. But if he went back, she might think he had bad intentions. He hadn't meant to catch her naked in the bathroom. He had no idea she'd take him up on his offer so quickly. He'd only been gone from the barn an hour. Maybe not even that long. She must have circled around after he drove off and gone into the apartment immediately. And why not? There was no electricity at the house. No hot water. She herself had expressed her doubts the water was safe.

He couldn't go back to the apartment.

He pulled his cell phone out of his pocket.

He was going to have to get Laura's house livable before he ended up having a mental meltdown.

"Harv? It's Bo. Listen. I got a big favor to ask."

Chapter Six

Jane swiped her palms down her blue jeans and waited at the front door of the Anderson mansion. Well, maybe it wasn't a mansion, but it was the biggest house she'd been invited to.

"Well, where are they? You think they changed their minds?" Laura asked. She stepped forward and pushed the doorbell again. "I don't hear anything. Maybe their doorbell doesn't work."

"Maybe it rings in another part of the house. Be patient."

Bo answered the summons wearing a canvas apron over a button-down and blue jeans. His sleeves were rolled up, attesting to the fact that he'd been in the middle of something. The flustered, whimpering man who had flinched from Jane's touch and ran out of his own apartment as if she were going to jump him was long gone. He smiled at each of them.

"Good evening, ladies. Come on in." He stepped back and opened the door wider.

"Bo, something smells good," Laura said walking into the foyer.

Jane followed her in and looked up at the chandelier hanging from the high ceiling.

"Are these marble floors?" Laura asked.

"No. Just tile made to look that way."

"Shows every speck of dirt, I bet. Seems like a poor choice for a farm family."

Jane cringed at Laura's criticism.

"No doubt. That's why I'm not allowed to enter through the front door, Miss Laura." Bo led them through the house into a cozy sitting room lined with bookshelves. "If y'all want to make yourselves comfortable, I need a few more minutes to get supper on the table. Can I get you something to drink?"

"Water," Laura said as she walked to the shelves and began reading titles on the spines of the books.

Jane turned to Bo and found him watching her.

"Jane?" he murmured. His gaze meandered over her for a few seconds, and Jane wondered if he was remembering this morning. If he screamed again, she'd have her answer.

I am not ashamed of my body. I will not be embarrassed.

She placed her hands on her hips and shifted on one foot. He blinked and met her gaze. The air crackled.

"What are my choices, Bo?"

He crooked his head at her. "Umm…well, there's tea and coffee and water, of course. Beer and muscadine wine, if you're a drinker."

"What is muscadine? I've never heard of it."

"It's a southern grape which grows wild around here."

Where Jane wondered. She didn't ask though. The whole naked in the bathroom thing had put them on shaky ground. She didn't want him to think she was asking for a tour of where the wild grapes grew.

"What are you having?"

His lips turned up in a smile. The sparkle in his blue eyes made her heart skip a beat or two. "I'll have whatever you're having."

"I'll try the wine."

"Great." He nodded and turned to go. Jane watched him leave. She pivoted to Laura who had pulled a book out and was reading the back of the dustcover. Where was Bo's mother? It seemed she should be here, but what did Jane know about etiquette? Laura took the book she held and sat down on the couch, and opening it, she began to read.

Jane walked out of the room and listened. She heard sound from down the hall and followed it. She found Bo pouring wine in a glass. He looked up as she entered. "Hi," he said. He handed her the glass. "Here you go."

Jane tasted it. "Whoa. It's sweet."

"You're in the Deep South. We like sweet." He opened a stainless steel, side-by-side refrigerator and placed the wine bottle inside. "Do you want to take this to Miss Laura?" He picked up a glass of ice water and held it out to her.

Jane smiled. "I like that."

"What? The wine?"

"No. The way you call her 'Miss Laura.'"

Bo raised an eyebrow. "She's my elder. I'm showing respect."

"Do you do that with men also?"

He bowed his head. "You know this is a matriarchal society, right?"

"No. I didn't know."

"Never doubt it." He growled it as he wiped his hands on a tea towel and stepped in front of the gas stove. He took a hot pad in his hand and lifted the lid from a Dutch oven. Picking up a wooden spoon, he stirred the contents in the iron pot.

Jane waited for him to say more, but he didn't, so she took Laura's water to her and came back to the kitchen. "Can I do anything to help?"

"Sure." He nodded to her to come closer. He turned his back to her, opened a drawer, and retrieved a spoon. He dipped it in the pot and held it out to her with one hand under the spoon to catch anything which dripped. "Taste this. Does it need anything?"

Jane hesitated for a moment. She looked at Bo. He shrugged. Jane grasped his wrist to steady it and accepted the spoon in her mouth. "Oh my goodness. That's very good."

"It doesn't need anything?"

Delicious. Hearty. Some kind of stew. It was tomato-based, she could tell that much. "No. It's perfect. What is it?"

"It's hominy slap stew."

"What's hominy?"

Bo shook his head. "It's what grits are made out of."

"Oh."

"You know what grits are, right?"

"I've heard of them. I watch movies."

Bo shook his head. "I'll try not to judge." He turned off the stove, wrapped the tea towel around his hands, and picked up the Dutch oven. "Do you mind putting that trivet on the table? I thought we'd eat in here. It's a little more comfortable than the dining room."

Jane picked up the wooden trivet from the counter and set it on the table next to the bay window. She saw three plates on the table. "Is your mother eating with us?"

"No. She's feeling under the weather." Bo set the iron pot on the table and went back to the counter. He scooped rice from a cooker into a serving bowl.

"Oh. Sorry to hear that."

"She may join us later if she starts to feel better. She's really not been herself since she choked the day you saved her."

"Anyone else would have done the same." Jane sipped the wine. The taste was growing on her.

"Except no one did." His serious expression made Jane pause. A lump rose in her throat. She turned away. The intensity on Bo's face was too much. Jane didn't really think his mother would have died if she hadn't been there. Knowing how to do the Heimlich was part of the training at the restaurant. The city had offered incentives to restaurants for all the staff who'd gone through emergency aid training.

Bo cleared his throat, and when Jane looked back at him, he was placing the rice on the table along with a bowl of salad and a basket of rolls. He stepped back and reaching behind him, he untied the apron and pulled it over his head. Moving to a long cabinet, he opened it to reveal a pantry. He hung the apron on a hook inside the door and closed it, and then he rolled his sleeves down and buttoned the cuffs. It was on the tip of Jane's tongue to make a quip about him covering up, especially considering how much he had seen of her earlier in the day, but she was still a little unsure about his reaction. She figured since he hadn't brought it up, neither should she.

He retrieved a wine glass and poured some wine from the open bottle on the counter. He swirled it around and took a sip before placing the glass next to a plate on the table.

"I think that's about everything. If you'd like to have a seat, I'll go get Miss Laura." He strode from the room, and Jane chose the chair to the right of his plate. This way, she wouldn't have to sit across from him as she ate. Laura could have that privilege. And if Jane was lucky, Laura and Bo would carry the conversation, and she could sit back and enjoy a meal in a real kitchen cooked on a real stove and served on really expensive china.

That is to say, real china.

Jane heard Laura's voice before they entered the room. She was talking about her eventful day at the house. Probably not as eventful as being caught naked in a man's bathroom, but Laura had gotten pretty worked up.

"So, how'd you get all those people out there today? I swear, it was like we were on one of those reality shows." Laura walked in first. "What do they call that show, Jane, where the people get their house overhauled?"

"*Home Wreckers?*" Jane suggested.

"Is that the name of it?"

Bo stepped to the table and pulled back a chair. He waited for Laura to sit down, and then he nudged it forward to the table.

"Anyhow, first the electrician showed up, then the plumber showed up, then a construction crew showed up and started looking at the foundation, and they didn't stop until they got to the roof."

Jane watched Bo's face as Laura talked. She was pretty sure he was behind all the activity that had occurred at Laura's house today. His expression didn't give anything away, however. He smiled and nodded politely in all the right places, refreshed her glass of water, then sat down himself. They passed the dishes around the table and doled out the food Bo had prepared. The aroma made Jane's mouth water, and she wasn't disappointed once they began to eat. As she hoped, Laura kept up the conversation until it took an unexpected turn about halfway through the meal.

"So, Bo. How come you acted so funny when you walked in on Jane butt naked this morning when she was taking a bath?"

Unfortunately, Bo had been in the middle of drinking from his glass. Instead of spewing the wine across the table, he choked on it and vacillated between coughing and gasping for air. Jane felt as if she were reliving the bathroom incident.

She bit her lip to keep the smile off her face as she waited for him to answer.

"I was not expecting Jane to be in the apartment. I certainly wouldn't have walked in the bathroom if I had known..." He glanced at her, his cheeks red, but whether it was embarrassment or from choking, she didn't know. "I'm sorry."

"I'm sorry too. I should have let you know I was there."

"Why didn't you lock the door?" Laura asked Jane. "Seems like if you don't lock it, you're just inviting someone to walk in on you."

"I didn't think he'd be back so quickly, Laura. I'm not used to locks on bathroom doors anyway since we didn't have one on the bathroom in our apartment at home, and we don't even have a door at the house here."

"You don't have a door?" Bo asked.

"Those nice men from the crew said they'd bring me one. Didn't they, Jane?"

Jane nodded and sipped the wine.

"They said the house was in really good shape to be as old as it is, and the roof has just a few places that need to be repaired. And they're going to fix the hole where the raccoons have been getting in, and the rotten wood at the front door. I told them they weren't allowed to cut down the tree though. I like that tree at the front steps. I think it adds character to the house."

"The tree is in the way," Jane said. "We can't even go in or out of the house without having to practically climb the thing."

"The tree stays," Laura said stubbornly. "I like it."

"Maybe they can find a way to build the front stairs around the tree," Bo suggested.

"Why don't we just cut a hole in the wall of the house and put the front door in a different place?" Jane said sarcastically.

"I like the tree."

"Yes, I know."

"Miles is a gifted craftsman. He will figure something out." Bo picked up the bottle and refilled his and Jane's glass.

****

The bell jangled on the door of *The Bread Basket* when Bo entered. Amber looked over her shoulder from where she appeared to be rolling biscuit dough.

"Howdy, stranger. Please tell me you brought me some tomatoes. I sold the last three yesterday."

Bo placed a peck basket on the counter in between them. "Yes. I got your text." Guilt niggled at him. Amber was supposed to be his girl, and she was supposed to have exclusive rights to him. That meant no other woman should know where the key to his apartment was, and no other woman should be bathing there, even if it was completely innocent.

At least it was innocent until he'd seen her breasts and hadn't been able to think of much else since.

Amber wiped her hands on the towel hanging from her waist and poured him a cup of coffee. "Can you stay for breakfast or do you not eat that meal anymore?"

More guilt. He used to come in every morning and eat breakfast while Amber got ready for the morning crowd. He lifted the baseball hat off his head and scratched his scalp. "I deserve that, I suppose." Oh, boy, did he.

"Well, it's okay, Bo. I mean, I didn't say it to make you

feel bad." She went into the kitchen, and in a moment, Bo smelled the sweet smell of French Toast Loaf, a specialty of Amber's. She came out and placed two pieces on a plate in front of Bo. "Here, sweetheart." She set napkin-wrapped silverware next to the plate.

Bo sighed, unwrapped the eating utensils, and cut a piece then stuffed it in his fat, horrible mouth. The caramelized sugar over the breaded loaf had a little party on his taste buds to a soundtrack of *jerk, jerk, you're a big jerk.*

He chewed the guilt and swallowed it. But it remained on his tongue. He risked a glance at Amber who had turned her back to him to work on the biscuit dough, but her eye caught him in the slanted mirror overhead.

"Have you met your cousin yet?"

"What?"

"Laura Justice and that girl who was with her who saved your mom from choking."

Bo dropped his eyes and ate another bite. *My, my.* If he was going to feel guilty, he sure as heck was going to enjoy Amber's cooking while he did it. She must have been unaware of his inner turmoil because she dusted her metal cutter with flour and pressed down on the batch of flattened dough.

What should he say?

Yes, yes, I met her and fondled her bare hip yesterday morning. I saw all parts usually covered up by underwear. I can wax poetic about the color of her nipples and have done so throughout the day. And, oh, would you like to know she has a mole on her lower—much lower—back?

"Yes, I met them both. They're staying in a little shack on what I thought was my back acreage until a few days ago. Now I know Laura Justice is my mother's second cousin, and she owns a thousand acres of our farmland and has owned it since before I was born."

"Shut up."

"It's the God's honest truth."

"Dang. You've had an eventful week." She rolled up the remaining dough, cut a few more biscuits then took the pan into the kitchen. She came back out with another batch of dough and began kneading it in her hands. Used to, watching her knead dough would turn him on. Bo assessed his mojo for a second or two.

Nope. Nothing.

He was in big trouble.

"So, whatchu gonna do about it?"

Huh?

She leaned against the back counter and watched him as she worked the dough. He'd been with her long enough to know she wouldn't be working biscuit dough that hard. Must be bread for lunch.

Could she know what was going on?

"What do you mean?"

"About Laura and her...who is that girl with her anyway?"

"Her daughter-in-law."

"Where's Laura's son?"

"He died in a fire along with Laura's husband."

"Sad. So they don't have anyone else, and they came here to live."

"It would appear that way."

"What are they going to do? Start farming?"

"I hope not. This is all so complicated. I can't believe my dad never told me about all of this. Didn't he know that eventually somebody from that family would come back to claim the land?"

"How could you not know about this, Bo?"

"You got me. Eric Jenters does all the accounting. He has to know about it, but I can't get in touch with him. He's on vacation."

"As much as I'm sure you pay him, you ought to have his cell number."

"Yeah, I guess."

The bell over the door jingled. Richard Cron walked in. He was a cattle farmer who headed up the livestock co-op for the county.

"Good morning, Richie. I've got some coffee here

waiting on you."

Bo nodded his head in Richard's direction. "Whatchasay, Richard?"

"Bo." Richard settled on the stool next to Bo and placed his cowboy hat on the chair on the other side of him.

Amber wiped her hands and went to the coffeemaker. Reaching for a large cup on a shelf in front of her, she poured coffee in it and set it on the counter. She bent down and pulled a small bowl out of the under-the-counter refrigerator. Picking up a spoon, she placed several dollops of cream in the coffee cup.

"Hey, what's that?" Bo asked.

"It's homemade cream. Richie likes it in his coffee, so I usually whip some up for him, don't I, darlin'?"

"You sure do. Nobody can whip cream like you, Amber."

She laughed and put the coffee in front of him. The cream piled high over the rim. Bo looked from Amber to Richard and back to Amber. She winked at him and stepped to the sink to wash her hands. For the first time since he walked in the diner, guilt took a backseat in his mind.

Next up? Jealousy. Richard was flirting with his woman, and she was flirting right back.

"How come I never got homemade whipped cream in a nice cup?" Bo asked.

"You don't like cream in your coffee, Bo. You drink it as black as the ace of spades. And this here mug is Richie's mug. He brought it from home 'cause he likes the way it handles. I get that, don't you?"

Bo had to give her that one. Still. How long had this been going on—*Richie* coming in and getting special treatment?

"Maybe everybody should bring their own cup in."

"Be okay with me as long, as it's dishwasher safe and they don't mind reminding me which one is theirs."

"That's a pretty good idea, Bo," Richard said and

slurped from his personal coffee cup. When he lowered the cup, he had a huge white dollop of cream on his moustache. He grinned at Bo, looking like an idiot.

Bo plucked a napkin from the holder and pushed it on the counter to him. "You have whipped cream on your face."

If anything, his grin got bigger. "What do you say, Amber?"

"I say if the cream is whipped well enough, it ought to peak well on moustache whiskers."

Bo laughed. "You people are making me sick to my stomach."

"Aww, it's just a little harmless fun."

Bo watched Amber's appreciative look she aimed at the cowman. Nope. He wasn't buying the harmless fun. "I didn't think the diner was open yet for breakfast."

"What? I let you in here. I can't very well kick Richie out."

"And besides, I supply her with all the milk she needs."

"You're the milkman? Since when?"

Bo looked at Richard and waited for his answer.

"Since I won the auction for all the milk cows from the 4-H kids. As long as the heifers are calving, and I got some surplus, I'm happy to supply Amber. I hate to see it go to waste."

"How many head?"

"Eighteen. I've got buyers for all the calves, and beef prices look like they're going up."

Amber placed a plate of whipped cream that may have had a large piece of French Toast Loaf underneath it in front of Richard. She held out a fork to him.

He grabbed the fork and had a hunk of the food in his mouth within seconds.

Richard's piece of loaf was a lot bigger than what Amber had served Bo. And she hadn't even given him the option of whipped cream on his, and he did like whipped cream, thank you very much.

"How come you handed him his fork?"

"Look at him eat. I tried giving him the wrapped silverware, but he doesn't bother to take off the napkin. I swear I've never seen a man love to eat like Richie Cron."

"Muhumphummph." Richard responded.

Bo shook his head in disgusted amazement. "Maybe I ought to go and leave you two alone."

Amber turned around and began to roll out the dough. She glanced up at Bo in the mirror. "Who? Richie and his breakfast? If you do, you'll miss the most entertaining spectacle of the day."

If not the most enlightening one, Bo thought, as he ordered a French Toast Loaf to go and attempted a gracious exit.

Chapter Seven

Do you want to come over for dinner?

Bo stared at the text from Amber. She'd obviously picked up on his jealousy and wanted to talk about it.

When did my life turn into a damn Lifetime movie? I don't even like that channel.

She'd want to meet early, which suited Bo fine. They both were early risers, which meant they went to bed with the proverbial chickens, though not with each other. Not for a while now.

Bo tried to think back to the last time he'd spent the night with her. Months, he was pretty sure. And she'd never spent the entire night with him. He'd convinced her early on to come out to the apartment at the barn, but she'd complained it was too far out and she didn't like having to get up even earlier to get breakfast ready at the diner instead of just walking downstairs from her loft over the restaurant.

Ordinarily, she closed at two in the afternoon, catering only to the breakfast and lunch crowd, unless someone called ahead of time. Once a month, she had a Friday night roast that drew a great crowd, especially the teens who had few options socially that didn't involve parking at the creek and getting in trouble. She opened the basement of the restaurant, which she had turned into a rec room of sorts, and they were allowed to stay until one in the morning if they cleaned up after themselves.

He texted back an affirmative and made a run through the fields. By the time he drove out to Laura's to drop off the breakfast loaf, the sun was already up in the sky, and men swarmed the dirt-packed yard like ants. Jane was at the side of the house on her knees putting order to a flowerbed while Miles Parker, a construction worker, stood nearby.

She wore cutoff jeans and a white T-shirt that brought out the coffee-and-cream complexion of her skin. Her black hair was braided, and she sat on her haunches and wiped her forehead as she listened to whatever tripe Miles was saying instead of doing the work he was supposed to be doing.

Bo walked to them. "Hi Miles. What're you doing?" *Other than not working, that is.*

"Oh, hey, Bo. I was just telling Jane here that she might not want to plant any vegetables this close to the house because of the lead paint."

"Lead paint?"

"Yeah. I can look at the sills and tell it's lead. That ain't good for the soil with the rain runoff. You eat lead in your vegetables, it's going to make you crazy."

Jane's brown gaze strayed to his, and she plucked up a dandelion plant bigger than her hand. He saw a quarter planter of tomato plants next to her in the dirt. Bo refrained from doling out any gardening tips or offering to bring her some tomatoes from his own garden. Instead, he held up the aluminum package.

"Good morning. Have you eaten breakfast?" he asked.

"Sure. Hours ago," Miles returned.

"Good to hear it, Miles. I was talking to Jane."

"Oh."

Jane smiled and unfolded her long legs to a standing position. She brushed the back of her jeans, which, Bo noticed, Miles watched with too much interest.

"See you later, Miles. Thank you for the advice," Jane said as she began to walk around to the front of the house.

"Sure thing, Jane. Say, are you free tonight?"

Are you kidding me? Anger rose in Bo's chest. What the heck was going on? Was every man in this county on the prowl? Bo watched Jane.

She paused and turned around, looking at Miles. "Free? Free for what?"

"To go get something to eat."

"Sure. What time should we be ready?"

"We?"

"Yeah. Laura and me."

Bo suppressed the chuckle blossoming in his chest.

Miles hopeful expression fell a bit. "Oh. Umm. Would Laura come too?"

"I can't leave her out here by herself."

"My truck only seats two. You sure she wouldn't mind if you just went out for a little while? We could bring her back something."

"I'll have to think about it, Miles. But thanks for asking me." She softened the rejection with a kind smile before turning on her heel and walking toward the tree in front of the door to the house. She looked up at Bo, and it was as if Miles never existed. "Would you like to come in? You have to use the tree for leverage to get on the porch."

Bo's throat closed up, and he swallowed. Such dedication to another person touched him, and Jane was loyal to a woman she wasn't even related to by blood. A furrow formed between her eyebrows.

"What's wrong?"

"Nothing's wrong."

"You don't want to climb a tree?" She rolled her eyes. "Honestly, I don't know why she cares so much about it when it's in the way." She ascended the stairs and grasped the tree as she edged by it. "I feel like I'm living in a funhouse."

"Because you're having fun?"

She shook her head. "Look at all these people."

She opened the weathered front door, and Bo followed her inside. The room was small. The women had placed a patio table and chairs on one side of the room and a couch and large television on the other. A camp stove sat on the counter next to the kitchen sink and an old refrigerator was pushed away from the wall.

"They're getting the house livable for you."

She knelt before a cooler, opened it, and retrieved two bottles of water. Walking to Bo, she handed him one of the bottles. Her dark eyes held a troubled look.

"What's wrong, Jane?"

"I didn't really think she meant it—about staying here. Living here."

"You can't be that opposed to the idea."

"Why do you say that?"

"Because you're planting tomatoes. When you plant, it's an act of faith because you're planning on being around when the tomatoes are ready."

"I got the biggest plants I could find. Even if we're not here, the deer will enjoy them." She reached her hand up to brush back a few strands of hair from her face. "And anyway, it was Laura's idea that I get some tomato plants. She is setting down roots here." Jane shook her head in disbelief.

"Her roots were already here," Bo reminded her gently.

"Yes. Yes, you're right. I just wish she wasn't going to so much trouble with the house and all."

"Getting the house fixed up wasn't her doing. It was mine. I sent the men here." Not that Bo was so sure that was a good idea with the way Miles was sniffing around like a dog that had caught a scent.

"Why? Why would you do all of this? Us being here has messed up your farm, your business. I know it has."

"I can't have you all living in a house that isn't safe. What if something happens?"

"Why do you care?"

A flash of her body exploded over his brain. *Because you were naked.*

Her eyes grew wide, and she threw her head back and laughed.

Had he said that out loud?

Man, I'm a dummy. "Umm. I brought you and Laura some breakfast. It's French Toast Loaf. Amber cooks it with bacon."

"Amber?"

"She's the owner of *The Bread Basket.*"

Jane unwrapped the aluminum foil. "She made French

Toast with bacon in it?"

"She's on a bacon bend right now. Everything has bacon in it."

"Yummy." Jane walked to the cabinet, opened a drawer, and pulled out a plastic knife and opened a cabinet and picked up two plastic plates. She came back to the table, cut two pieces off the loaf, and placed them on the plates. "Want to sit down?"

"Where's Laura?"

"She's on the roof supervising the workers."

"Are you kidding?"

"The guys promised me they'd watch her really closely."

The guys.

In less than two days, it seemed that *the guys* had gotten mighty chummy with his new neighbors. The temptation to stay was really strong, even though he had a full day's work waiting for him. If he was going to knock off early to go to Amber's, he needed to get going. He'd noticed the beans in the east pasture weren't thriving as they should, and if they didn't get some rain in the next week, he was afraid he was going to lose the whole crop. The forecast didn't even promise a cloud in the sky. The egg production was down in the henhouse, and Bo suspected a snake was getting in there and eating them. If not a snake, a raccoon. He needed to investigate to see if he could figure out the culprit.

"I'm sorry. I'd like to—"

A knock sounded on the door and Miles stepped in. "Hey, Bo. Jane, I've got some really nice stone you could line your beds with. They're left over from landscaping of a house we were working on last week. If you like, I could bring them to you."

"That's so nice of you. Thank you." She smiled at him, and jealousy burned in Bo's chest.

Miles preened under Jane's attention, and Bo felt like going over there and punching him a couple of times. Miles back-stepped onto the porch. "I better get back to work." He glanced at Bo. "I'll see you in a bit."

"Sure."

The door closed. Jane turned to him, the smile still on her face. "What were you saying?"

"That I'd love to sit down for a few minutes." He claimed one of the chairs, feeling triumphant that he was in here and Miles was not.

Jane sat down on the chair at the corner next to his and pulled one of the plates toward her. "Thank you for dinner last night. It was a treat. I think Laura enjoyed herself a lot."

"I'm glad."

She took a bite of a piece of the loaf. "Oh, wow. This is really good."

Bo bit into the other piece. His second breakfast of the day. If he didn't watch it, he was going to need a nap before lunch.

"I'll make sure Laura returns your book."

"It was my dad's. I'm not sure it will get read again, so she's welcome to keep it as long as she likes."

Jane pursed her lips. "I won't tell her that. She has a really bad habit of hoarding books, and we've already accumulated enough stuff since we've been here that we'll have to rent a U-Haul if we ever go back. Or just leave it, which wouldn't be fair to you."

"Why wouldn't it? It's not my house. It's not my stuff to clean up."

Her lips turned up in a sardonic smile. "I think we both know that whether it's yours or not, it falls to you to clean up."

Her insight made him pause. He put the fork down, noticing as he did so his plate was empty.

"Am I right?"

"I'm not admitting anything." He stood up. "I better go. Forgive me for pulling the whole eat-and-run routine." He picked up the plate and looked around. "Where's your garbage?"

Jane pointed to a garbage can in the corner.

"What are you guys doing with your garbage?"

"I've been hauling it to the dumpster at the edge of town."

"If you like, you can leave it at the road on Thursday, and I'll take it when I take mine from the apartment."

"Okay. Thank you."

Bo walked to the door. "Enjoy the rest of your breakfast. Don't give any to Miles. He needs to be doing more working and less socializing."

****

That evening he sat across from Amber at her table. Country music played low from some electronic device in the corner, and she'd put the red veil on the lamp, which meant Bo could get lucky if he was so inclined. It was tempting to stay, because MayLynn had yet to make nice with him. She'd been gone when he stopped at home to check on her and hadn't returned his texts until he threatened to call Caden and report her car stolen and her kidnapped.

I'm fine, she'd texted back.

And that was the *I'm fine* answer women, including his mother, used when they were really pissed. He'd let it go, deciding to give her space to cool off. Staying the night with Amber would give MayLynn that space. He'd dressed the part, going to the trouble of ironing a knit shirt.

Still.

If he were honest with himself—and with Amber—this needed to be a break-up dinner. And he wanted to be classy about it. But he was nervous because he really liked Amber, he just hadn't been in love with her for a while, and he didn't want to lose the friendship they had fallen into. He valued her in his life, and he wanted to keep her here if he could.

She'd fixed country-fried steak, his favorite, along with field peas, mashed potatoes, and fresh yeast rolls, and it was only his mama's stern upbringing that kept him from picking up the plate and licking every speck of homemade gravy from it. However, it didn't keep him from wiping the plate clean with the roll and eating it.

"That was delicious. Thank you," he said wiping his mouth with the cloth napkin she'd provided.

"Want another beer?"

"I better not." Since he wasn't staying.

She picked up his plate and stacked it on top of hers then pushed them to the side. Placing her elbows on the table, she tented her hands and gave him an assessing stare. "Want to tell me what's going on?"

Bo folded his arms over his chest. "What do you mean?"

"I don't like games. You know that."

Bo shrugged his shoulders. "What games?"

"What was with your behavior this morning in the diner?"

Oh. That.

"I just found it really interesting how Richard Cron comes in drooling all over you and doesn't even try to hide it."

"He is a drooler, but it's the food he likes. Not me."

"Come on. You're not that gullible, are you?"

"I've known him my whole life. He had plenty of chances to catch me before I got married, and he wasn't interested."

"You're not married now."

"No, I'm not."

Her statement hung in the air. Bo watched her to determine her meaning. She returned his gaze. It became a contest, and Bo was the first one to look away.

He scooted his chair back. "Don't let me hold you back."

"Are we done? Is that what your pissing contest this morning was about?"

Bo sighed. "I didn't pick a fight with Richard."

"You tried."

"He has the manners of a pig."

"He's funny, and besides, it's my diner, and no one else was in there. If he wants to be a little goofy, especially if it's about my cooking, I'm okay with that. And I think it's ridiculous that you're jealous."

"Do I need to be?"

She shrugged. "Yeah. Maybe a little, but you and I are exclusive, and I wouldn't cheat on you, Bo."

"What's that mean? We're barely involved as it is. If I don't come in to the diner, I don't see you at all."

"I'm a business owner. If I'm not here, nothing happens."

"Yeah, well, I run a farm, and I make the time to see you."

"Not so much anymore, as I've noticed."

"I like you, Amber, but..." Bo shook his head as he searched for words. "You never want to go much further than my occasional nights over here. That's not a relationship."

"I like my life as it is. I tried marriage. It didn't work out."

"But that wasn't your fault. Your ex-husband was a jerk."

"Yes, he was, but I don't want to get married again."

"Is this all you're willing to do? A good meal and roll in the hay when you get the occasional itch? I don't want to be friends with benefits. It feels inauthentic."

"What are you saying? You're ready to get married and settle down? Really? With me here in my loft?"

"So, getting married to you means I'd have to live here in this closet."

"I'd rather live in this closet than your attic in the barn or, God forbid, with your crazy mother."

Ouch. He glared at her, but there was nothing repentant about her when she arched an eyebrow at him.

"That isn't very nice."

"Come on, Bo. This is me you're talking to. We both know how your mom is. If you want to get married, then you're going to have to cut the apron strings."

Bo stood up and stalked to the door. He opened it and exited her apartment. "I don't live with my mother. Well, I do, but not like you mean. I take care of her, and there isn't anything wrong with that."

Amber followed him down the outside stairs that led down the side of the restaurant. "Oh, give me a break. Who does your laundry, huh? When's the last time you cooked your own supper?"

"I cooked last night as a matter of fact, and my mother wasn't even there." He stalked toward the front where he had parked his truck and stopped short. There stood Jane in front of her car, which was parked next to his.

"Which explains why you were cooking, I bet," Amber yelled. She probably hadn't expected Bo to stop suddenly because she ran into his back. "Ooph."

"Hi," Jane said. Her eyes strayed to Amber. "I…didn't realize you weren't open for supper. I was hoping to get something to go."

"Oh." Amber stepped around Bo. "Yeah. I only do suppers for special orders ahead of time. Sorry."

Jane's expression was pensive. *Dammit.* She must have heard him and Amber arguing.

"Tell you what. Let me grab my keys, and I can get you something. It'll be leftovers though. Do you mind?" Amber headed up the stairs and spoke over her shoulder.

That was Amber for you. Ever the business owner. She wasn't going to turn away a customer, even if that customer was interrupting a break-up fight.

"Leftovers would be great."

Jane wouldn't meet his eyes; instead, she stared at the gravel parking lot.

Dammit. Dammit. Dammit.

Bo searched his brain for something to say. He opened his mouth. "Did Laura make it down from the roof?"

"Yes."

Stupid. Stupid. Stupid.

"Is everything okay?" he asked.

"I think so," she said quietly. "I probably wouldn't have stopped here, but I saw your truck and I thought…."

Dammit. Dammit. Dammit.

Amber jogged down the stairs. "I've got some

meatloaf, beans, and twice baked potatoes. Will that do?" She went to the front door and unlocked it. "I'm Amber Fellows. I didn't catch your name."

"Jane Stanford."

"She'll need it heated up," Bo offered.

Amber glared at Bo. "I don't send cold food out to my customers." She turned to Jane. "Come on in, Jane. It'll just take me a few minutes to get it ready for you, okay?"

"Okay."

That appeared to be Bo's cue to leave.

Great. The woman he'd last slept with was getting all chummy with the woman he'd last seen naked.

The urge to stay and monitor the conversation, perhaps steer it to safer topics like the weather or…religion was nearly as strong as the urge to escape.

Nearly.

Chapter Eight

Jane watched through the plate glass window as Bo's truck headlights came on and he backed his truck out of the parking lot.

Well, this was interesting.

Apparently, Bo and Amber were involved, and Jane had just witnessed the tail end of an argument.

No, I interrupted their argument. Questions burned on her tongue, but she refrained from asking.

"Do you want enough for two?"

Jane turned around and saw Amber coming through a swinging door with several ceramic containers. She lined the containers on the counter.

"Yes. Thank you."

"Can I fix you some coffee or tea while you wait?"

"I'd love some tea."

Amber washed her hands at the sink next to the wall. She opened a refrigerator, retrieved a pitcher, and poured some in a plastic tumbler. She set it in front of a swiveled stool at the counter.

Jane took the seat. She remembered the tea from the day she and Laura had eaten here. Bringing the cup to her lips, she drank. The tea was cold and sweet. Delicious.

Amber crouched behind the counter and set two plates on its surface. "Bo tells me you and he are neighbors."

"My mother-in-law grew up in a little house not too far from him."

"Huh." She spooned food on the plates. "I'm sending these plates with you. No hurry getting them back. Just whenever you're done with them and back this way."

"All right. Thanks."

"You think you two will stay here for a while?"

"Laura seems to want to."

"You don't."

"If she wants to stay here, then of course, I will stay here too. We're family, and that means a lot to me."

"Really?"

"Yes. I never knew my parents. I grew up in foster care. When I married Mandy, his parents treated me as if I was their daughter. They're the only family I've ever known. Mandy and his father died the same night. Laura and I only have each other, so if she stays, I stay. And if she goes, I go too. That's what families do. At least, that's how I imagined families acting."

"What kind of work did you do before y'all moved here?"

"I was a waitress."

Amber wrapped the plates in aluminum foil and placed them in a paper bag with handles at the top. "Oh yeah?"

Jane nodded and sipped her tea.

"I suppose you'll be looking for a job if you all settle here, unless you and Laura are going to try your hand at farming." She placed napkins and flatware in the bag.

"I can't really see that happening."

"Oh, you never know. Maybe Bo could teach you all how to farm. He likes to be helpful. It's one of his downfalls, actually."

Jane didn't reply.

"I guess you heard us arguing."

"It's none of my business really."

Amber snorted. "I can sure tell you're not from around here. People in this town think everything is their business. We probably wouldn't have taken our fight outside except the downtown rolls up the sidewalks at eight o'clock. We didn't think anyone was around to hear. Bo's a good guy. I'm the problem. Not him."

"I'm sure you two will work it out."

"We'll see. Well, here's your food."

Jane stood up and pulled some money out of her pocket. "How much?"

"No charge."

"Of course, I'm going to pay. You went to all this trouble."

"Look. You saved MayLynn's life in here the other day. If someone dies in my diner—well, that's bad for business, so just consider this my thank you."

"That's very kind of you."

"And don't be a stranger. You and your mother-in-law come in for lunch again."

Jane gripped the handles of the bag with one hand and supported the weight of the bag with the other. She liked Amber Fellows a lot. She didn't want to like her since finding out Amber was Bo's girlfriend, but how could she not like her? She was as friendly and down to earth as anyone Jane had ever met. She was also an excellent cook and ran a clean and efficient restaurant. Jane had worked in enough restaurants to know a savvy restaurant owner when she met one. The free meal Amber had handed her wasn't simply a thank you for Jane's act the other day. It was a welcome to the neighborhood gesture. That's how one built a customer base. And it was very smart.

She drove back to the house, passing Bo's pecan-groved driveway on the way. From the road, she could barely see the lit house through the trees. It was silly of her to have thought he wasn't attached. If he wasn't married or involved with someone, then there was probably something wrong with him.

And what did it matter anyway? Sure, she was attracted to him, but it hadn't occurred to her that anything would come from it.

Yeah, Sure, Jane Doe Stanford. Who are you trying to fool?

That morning when they'd sat next to each other on the rock, she had acknowledged the attraction she felt. She'd felt the pull of him and wondered what it would be like to lean forward and taste the coffee on his lips. Yesterday, she'd climbed back in the tub and imagined a few bathroom scenarios that didn't end with him slamming the door and running away. His reaction made more sense now that she knew about Amber.

Jane pulled the car next to the house and cut the engine. Thanks to the workers, they had electricity in part of the house provided by a generator that had just appeared, a loaner from Bo, one of them had told her. Light shone through the windows, and even though they didn't have any appliances plugged in since the electrician hadn't rewired the kitchen yet, they did have lamps in the main room, the bedroom, and the bathroom.

She carried the food bag inside the house. Laura wasn't in the room. "Laura?"

No answer.

Jane glanced in the bathroom as she walked by then went into the bedroom. From the floor lamp in the corner they'd purchased from the furniture store downtown, Jane saw Laura was already in bed. She bent over the woman who was breathing evenly in her sleep and placed a hand on her forehead. Laura's eyes flickered open.

"Are you feeling okay?"

"Yes. Just tired, and we still don't have a television."

Jane sat on the edge of the bed, and Laura rolled on her side and propped the pillow behind her head. "What about the book you borrowed from Bo?"

"Finished it."

"I could go borrow some more books."

"I don't really feel like reading."

"Perhaps climbing all over the roof was too much," Jane said.

"Maybe, but I wanted to be sure they were doing a good job."

"I've got us some supper, and it smells really good."

"I'm not hungry."

"You didn't eat any lunch, and I drove all the way into town to get us something to eat."

Laura sighed. "I'm supposed to be the mother figure here."

"Please?"

"Can we eat it in here?"

"We can do whatever we want, as long as it's eating

supper."

Laura didn't protest, so Jane took that as acquiescence. She hopped up and retrieved the food. When she came back to the bedroom, Laura had propped herself against the headboard of the bed. The meal was quiet, and Jane noticed Laura mostly picked at her food.

Something was wrong. It wasn't like to Laura not to argue with Jane about anything, and it also wasn't like her to lie in the bed and not eat. She hadn't felt hot when Jane had touched her earlier. What could it be?

"You didn't fall while you were coming down from the roof, did you?"

"No."

Jane waited for her to snap at her, but she didn't. Jane watched the older woman move the food around the plate. Finally, she set it aside.

"Thanks. That was good."

"How do you know? You barely tasted it."

"I ate enough. It's nice to have light, isn't it?"

The comment was so unusual for Laura, fear rose inside of Jane. *She's trying to distract me. She's hiding something. But what? What could be wrong?*

Jane knew the woman well enough not to push her too much about it. She cleared away the food and plates and left her alone to rest. Later that night, Jane settled in her own bed, all of the events of the day running through her mind.

Bo had a girlfriend who owned *The Bread Basket*. He and Amber had had a fight about Bo and his close relationship with his mother. Amber didn't really think the close mother/son relationship was as much of a problem as Amber's own issues about it. Or was Amber, out of loyalty to Bo, just saying that to Jane because she knew Jane had overheard the argument?

Jane sighed and plumped her pillow then lay on her stomach.

What did any of it matter? As Jane herself had told Amber, it wasn't her business. The exchange had meant to be private.

And maybe it really was for the best that Jane had heard it. Otherwise, she would have gone on thinking Bo was available…

…when he wasn't.

****

"How was your vacation, Eric?" Bo asked, sitting down on the chair across from his accountant's desk.

Eric's eyebrows rose far above the frame of his eyeglasses. "Now, Bo, we both know you're not here to find out how many fish I caught in Alaska."

Bo laughed, a little uneasily. "You know why I'm here?"

"I'd say it has something to do with Laura Stanford staying in the house she grew up in."

"Did you know her?"

"Well, sure. Not real well, of course, but I knew her mom and dad. Her mom and I graduated high school together."

Bo searched the other man's expression for any sign he had been hiding something all these years. "She owns a fourth of our land."

"Right."

"Right? You knew about this?"

"Sure. Your dad set it up years ago. I also direct deposit a percentage of the profit from the thousand acres, as is required on the agreement."

Bo stood up. "How come I never knew about this?"

Eric made an *I dunno* sound. "I figured your dad told you."

"He didn't."

"Didn't you ever wonder how come the percentage was taken out?"

"I never paid that much attention. You're the bookkeeper. I figured you handled the accounts."

"I do and make sure the taxes and bills are paid."

"It never occurred to you to tell me? Three hundred of those acres are for gourmet herbs. That's almost a third more per acre profit than my soybeans."

Eric shrugged his shoulders. "I didn't tell you where to plant your rosemary and basil."

"Geez, Eric. I'm running that farm. I ought to be in the know about these things. What else are you keeping from me?"

He shrugged again. "I'm not deliberately keeping anything from you. Any changes that have been made to the farm have been made by you. Anything you ask me, I'll tell you if I know, but I just figured when you took over after Zachary died you knew all you needed to know."

"Do you know why my dad would have sold the land to Isaiah Justice for ten cents an acre and why my dad would treat the land as his own and send Mr. Justice a percentage of the profits after he moved away? Or why Mr. Justice would move away when he just bought a big chunk of land for nearly nothing?"

The older man blinked at him like a wise owl.

"Do you know?"

He moved his head slowly from side to side. Going to a filing cabinet, he opened the top drawer, flipped through some hanging folders, and withdrew several. Placing them on his desk, he thumbed through them. "Your dad worked out the agreement with Isaiah Justice then gave me the bookkeeping to figure out. I didn't ask him why, and he never told me."

He picked up a stapled paper and handed it to Bo, all without making eye contact.

"Why don't you just tell me what you're not telling me?"

"Because I don't jibber-jabber. You want that kind of mess, talk to my wife."

"What's her number?"

Eric chuckled. "She doesn't know jibber-jabber from that far back. She's from Oxford, Mississippi, and has only been living here five years."

"I thought your wife was from Athens, Georgia."

"That was my first wife. Patty is wife number three."

Eric's mouth widened in a grin that would put the Cheshire cat to shame.

"Are you an SEC fan?"

"College football is my religion."

"Where was your second wife from—Tuscaloosa or Auburn?"

He held up a finger and wagged it at Bo. "Jibber-jabber. I don't do it."

****

Jane didn't go to the barn for a bath, nor did she go to Hesed Rock for any dawn conversations with Bo over coffee. She walked to his house later in the morning when she was sure he would be out in the fields working. She had the book in her hand that Laura had borrowed from Bo. She hoped if Bo's mother was home, Jane could borrow a few more.

Jane stood on the front porch and pushed the doorbell. In a few minutes, MayLynn Anderson opened the door, a cold expression on her face.

"Yes?"

"Hello, Mrs. Anderson. My name is Jane Stanford."

Something flashed in her eyes.

"We met at *The Bread Basket*. Well, we sort of met. Not formally, I suppose."

MayLynn nodded. "Of course. Thank you for..." She sighed angrily. "Do you mind going around the house and meeting me on the back patio? I'll bring some tea out there, and you can tell me what your business is."

"Oh, I'm sorry. I don't want to impose." Jane held the book out. "You're busy, I'm sure. I just wanted to return this."

"I owe you a glass of tea, at least."

"No, that's...."

MayLynn stepped back, and the door slid shut with a soft click.

"Oookay then." Jane stepped off the porch and followed a narrow paved walk around the corner of the house.

This ought to be fun.

There was a large hedge that met the back corner of the house. An elaborate wooden arched arbor formed a doorway through the bushes. Jane walked through it and stepped onto a stone patio lined with the most incredible flowers Jane had ever seen. She walked over to the plants, some of which were taller than she was and—oh, the colors, ranging from white and pink to nearly black. A few of the flowers she could identify—the daisies and tiny roses, something else that looked suspiciously like saffron. Many of the flowers were deep rich colors, and the blooms were bigger than her head. Obviously, Mrs. Anderson had a thumb as green as the leaves on the flowers.

The back door swung open, and she walked out with a tray. "Come on, then," she said setting the tray on the table. "Do you like sweet tea?"

Jane approached the table. "Yes, ma'am."

MayLynn arched an eyebrow at Jane. "Stop loitering. Sit down."

Jane placed the book on the table and settled on a chair.

"What's that?"

"It's a book…" Jane hesitated. Laura had inferred that MayLynn didn't like her; so to be safe, Jane decided not to bring the other woman up. "A book Bo let me borrow."

MayLynn looked at the cover then at Jane. It was a book about the Indian Revolution, not anything Jane herself would choose to read.

Please don't quiz me on it.

MayLynn picked up the glass and handed it to her. "Thank you for your…help the other day."

"You're welcome."

"Where did you learn to do that?"

"I took a CPR class shortly after my husband died."

"Did he have a heart attack?"

"No. He died in a fire."

"My husband died of a cardiac arrest. He was in the field when it happened. We didn't find him for a couple of hours probably. There wasn't any hope by the time we found him."

"It's hard when you don't get to say goodbye."

"Yes, it is."

They sat for a few moments. A wind chime hanging from the eave of the house broke the silence as a light breeze blew.

A rooster crowed in the distance. MayLynn clicked her tongue. "Those are Bo's chickens, and one rooster has no idea that his crowing is supposed to be reserved for after daybreak."

Jane laughed. "Is it all day?"

"Pretty much, yes. Extremely annoying. I'll be glad when Bo takes him to Amber for chicken salad."

Jane shivered. "I've never seen a live chicken before."

"You're not missing anything. They're horrible animals. They'll eat anything, and they're mean. Woe to any bird who shows weakness. The others will pull out her feathers and peck her to death if given the chance."

"Yuck. Really?"

"Yes. I don't eat chicken on principle, except for Amber's chicken salad and that's only because she's such a good cook. A chicken attacked me when I was a child, and since then, I don't want to be around them. I don't like to see them or hear them."

"A chicken attacked you?"

"A rooster. Spurred me from neck to ankle. Unprovoked. I told Bo I didn't want any chickens around here, so he made a pen down past the storage house. There are a few trees there, so they roost at night if need be. It keeps them somewhat safe from the foxes and coyotes." MayLynn took a long pull from her tea glass. "Tell me what brings you here."

"I wanted to bring the book—"

MayLynn shook her head. "Not today. To Haven. To that old shack out there in the middle of nowhere."

"Oh." Jane straightened. "My mother-in-law, Laura Justice Stanford, grew up there."

MayLynn went motionless.

"I thought you probably knew that."

She nodded once, her intense blue eyes watching Jane. "She has never come back until now."

Jane shook her head. "She hasn't really told me much about her life here before, except that the house was her family's. Since her husband and my husband, her son, died in the fire, she's never been the same. But now that she's here, it's like part of her has come back to life. She's happier than I've seen her in long time."

"But you all aren't planning on staying."

It wasn't exactly a question but close enough that Jane was compelled to answer.

"I didn't think so at first, but Laura seems to want to."

"That dilapidated old house should have been torn down years ago."

Jane watched the glass sweat, condensation running down the side and onto the tabletop. "Perhaps. But Bo has been very helpful with arranging for workers to come out to get the electric back on and make sure the water is potable. There's even a construction crew which is helping with some of the structure of the house that wasn't sound."

"Oh, Bo." The sadness in those two words caused Jane to focus on the woman across the table from her. MayLynn had turned aside. She was looking across the patio to her flowers. "I asked him to take care of things. I trusted him to do that...and he has."

"Yes. He's been very kind."

"Just like..." MayLynn swallowed then cleared her throat. "His father. His father was an incredibly kind man."

"I'm sorry I never knew him."

MayLynn's gaze came back to her. "Yes, well." A briskness entered her tone. "What doesn't kill us makes us stronger, so they say."

"Do you believe that?" Jane asked.

Jane waited to see if the other woman would answer her question.

MayLynn looked down to her lap. "No," she said after

a moment. "I feel much weaker since Zachary died. I don't breathe as well, as if it nearly hurts to take in too much air, as if…part of my breath went with him when he breathed his last. It sounds silly, I know."

"No, it doesn't." The silence stretched between them. "May I tell you something very personal?"

MayLynn studied her for a long time before she nodded her head slowly.

"I remember the last time Mandy and I made love. I've thought about it many times, because I had just finished a double shift at the restaurant, and I was taking a trip the next day, and I remember thinking I was really tired, and I loved him, but just hurry up so I can go to sleep, you know? But if I had known that it was going to be the last time, the very last time to have him inside me, to feel his skin, and his lips on mine, I would have appreciated it more. Even though I would have been sad, I would have paid closer attention."

A tear fell from MayLynn's eye and trailed down her cheek. She reached up and swiped it with the finger that still held her wedding and engagement rings.

"I hope I didn't offend you by telling you that. I've never shared that with anyone else because it is so personal. It just seems like when something so awful happens, it makes you realize how precious life is. And it's sad, because often what you realize you had can't ever be brought back again."

The sounds of the day filled the air between them, and the rooster crowed once more. This time, MayLynn didn't even seem to notice.

"I've never seen flowers so beautiful," Jane commented. "What are they?"

"You must be referring to my dahlias." For the first time, MayLynn smiled, and Jane recognized the same shape of Bo's lips when he smiled.

"The large ones?"

"Yes. I've won awards with them."

"I'm not surprised. You must spend a lot of time out

here."

"Yes, I do."

"Is it all right if I take a closer look?"

"Let me show you."

They left their drinks on the table and for the next hour, Jane accompanied MayLynn through the flower garden and listened as the older woman talked about her passion for her flowers. Before Jane left, she had a basket full of cut flowers and several glass vases with more flowers arranged just so. She was about halfway down the road, when Bo's truck pulled up next to her. He rolled his window down, and the shock on his face was priceless.

"You've talked to my mother, I see."

"Yes."

He shook his head staring at the basket then raised his gaze to Jane. "What did you say to her?"

"Nothing special, really."

"Nothing special, really." His disbelieving tone made her chuckle. "Can I give you a ride? I assume you're going home."

Home.

The little shack was beginning to feel more like home.

Jane circled the truck, and putting the basket on the seat and pushing it toward Bo, she climbed inside.

Bo shifted the truck and it began to move along the road. "I can't believe she gave you cut flowers and even arranged them for you."

"Well, she arranged one vase. I did the other one."

"You did…?"

"She showed me how to do it."

"She showed you how to arrange her flowers?" He raised one hand from the steering wheel in a gesture of surrender.

"Bo, your mother is sweet once she warmed up to me. She loves her flowers, obviously, so I expressed my appreciation, and she liked that."

"Unbelievable."

He pulled the truck up to the house and peered

through the windshield, a quizzical expression on his face. "Do you all have electricity yet?"

"Sort of. We are using your generator a few hours a day in half of the house. The electrician is rewiring the house and the kitchen is complicated, he told me."

Bo's mouth thinned. "Who's the electrician?"

"Tony Something."

"Tony Witherspoon."

"Yes, that's him. Why? Is something wrong with him?"

Bo mumbled a few words under his breath.

"What?"

"Nothing."

"We really appreciate you letting us use the generator."

"What about water?"

"Gus replaced some of the pipes, but they had to tear the floor up to do it, so Miles is working on the floor in my bedroom."

"Uh-huh."

Jane studied Bo's tense expression.

"What is it?"

Bo shook his head. "Just ignore me, Jane. It's stupid, I know. I feel…a little protective is all. You and Laura being out here all by yourselves, and now half the male population in the county knows it."

"You think it's something I ought to be concerned about?"

"Probably not, and you could call me, couldn't you, if you needed to?"

"I could, yes."

"Let me give you my cell number."

Jane pulled her cell phone from her pocket and unlocked it. She opened the contacts file, and Bo recited his number to her. "Why don't you call me, then I'll have yours."

She called the number he had given her and waited. It rang in her ear, but Jane didn't hear it ring in the cab of the truck.

"Oh, dang it," Bo said.

"What is it?"

"I don't have my cell phone."

"Where is it?"

Bo didn't answer.

"Do you remember?"

"Yeah, I think so."

Bo's voice sounded in her ear. "Hi. This is Bo. Leave me a message, and I'll get back to you." A beep sounded. Jane cut her eyes to the man beside her.

"Help! I've been kidnapped by a man who doesn't know where his phone is. He says I can call him if I need to, but he won't answer his phone!" Jane held the cell phone in front of her and touched the screen to disengage the call.

Bo grinned. "Point taken, Miss Jane Smarty Pants. Sorry. I'll find it and call you later, all right?"

"Okay. Do you want to come in?"

"Thanks. Another time."

Jane examined Bo's profile. He drummed his fingers on the steering wheel. Was he embarrassed he'd offered to help her out, then realized he didn't even have his phone?

She unbuckled her seat belt and opened the door. Taking the basket MayLynn had loaned her, she hooked the handle over her arm. "Thanks for the ride, Bo."

"You're welcome. Oh." He snapped his fingers. "I almost forgot. I brought something for the house. It's in the back of the truck."

Jane looked in the bed of the truck. "What is it?" A box was back there. Jane looked closer. It was a… She clapped her hands. "Is it really?"

"An air conditioner. It's just a window unit, but as small as the house is, it's probably powerful enough to keep you cool no matter where you are."

"My gosh. That's wonderful." Already, Jane was looking forward to the cool air.

"Want me to bring it inside? I can hook it up for you."

"Sure. Let me just check on Laura and be sure she's okay with you coming inside." Jane smiled sweetly in case her words might hurt his feelings. "Sometimes she sleeps on the couch. I don't want to catch her unaware."

Jane walked up on the porch and placed the basket behind the tree before opening the door. Laura must have been in the bathroom because the door was closed. Jane knocked on the door. "Hi. I'm back. Are you in there?"

"Yes."

"Is it all right if Bo comes in? He brought us an air conditioner to put in the window."

"Tell him to come back later."

"Are you okay?"

Laura waited a couple of seconds before she responded. "I'm just not up for company. Those men have been in here all day. I want some peace and quiet. He'll get that, I'm sure. He's from the country."

Disappointment filled Jane's chest. "All right." She went back outside. Bo was already at the bottom of the porch stairs.

"I'm sorry," she said. "She's tired. I'm really sorry because I'd like to use it."

"I can come back."

Jane opened the door and stepped out of the way. "Why don't you just set it inside the door. We can get to it later."

With seemingly little effort, Bo traversed the stairs, stepped around the tree, and brought the large box inside the room. He crouched down and gently placed it on the floor to the right of the doorway. Then he straightened. He glanced briefly around the room then stepped back outside. Jane followed him out. They went around the tree and into the yard. Bo turned to her. "I'll probably stay out at the barn tonight if you want to call me."

"Will you have your phone?"

He tucked his head bashfully. "I hope so. I'm going to go look for it now."

She reached forward and placed her hand on his forearm. "Thank you, Bo. I appreciate so much everything you've done for us."

He nodded at her, and his mouth crooked up on one side in a small smile. "My pleasure, ma'am."

Goose bumps arose on her skin at the soft tone of his voice and the warm gaze he was aiming her way.

He belongs to Amber.

****

Bo stood on Amber's porch and knocked on her door. Richard Cron's milk van sat outside of the restaurant in the late afternoon sunlight. Bo had parked right next to it, since Richard was in the spot he usually used when he was paying a social call. Jealousy burned his craw.

Stop it. You were planning on breaking up with her anyway.

Amber opened the door, her eyes roved over his face. "I guess I'm busted, huh?"

Bo couldn't help it. He smiled, and the jealousy dissipated like cigarette smoke on a breeze. "Well, you're dressed at least. Is he?"

Amber looked behind her. "Hey, Richie. Bo wants to know if you're still dressed."

Richard walked up behind Amber, his brows creased in concern, maybe even a little guilt.

"Hey, Bo."

"Richie," Bo returned using Amber's shortened version of his name.

"I was just...uh...delivering some milk."

Amber glared at him. "No, you weren't."

His eyes went wide. "Did I not bring you some milk up here?"

"Well, yeah, but that wasn't really why you came here. Geez."

"It most certainly was."

Amber put her hand on her hip and shook her head at him. "How gullible do you think Bo is? If you had wanted to deliver milk, you would have done it this morning."

Richard blinked at her. "It's goat milk. I didn't have it this morning."

"You seriously came here to bring me goat's milk." Her tone of voice displayed her irritation. "I hope you don't expect Bo to believe that."

"I might believe it," Bo said. "But I don't think Amber does, Richard."

"If you just came here to bring me goat's milk, why the heck didn't you wait and bring it tomorrow?"

"It's fresh."

"Then why did you come in the apartment?"

"Well…" Richard shrugged. "You invited me, and you had pie."

Amber sighed. "Oh, dammit, Richie,"

"Listen, I don't want to interrupt the love spat. I just want to pick up my phone. I think I left it here…" He glanced at Richard. "Last night."

"Oh, yeah. You did." Amber's anger disappeared. "I gave it to your mom. She came by for lunch."

"All right." Bo stepped back and took hold of the railing. "See you later."

"Wait a minute," Amber said. "You got any early corn you could bring by in the morning? I'd really like to make creamed corn for lunch."

"Yeah. I can get you some."

"Okay." She looked back at Richie then at Bo. "Are we cool?"

"You mean, are we still friends?"

"Yes, that's what I mean."

"Lord, I hope so. I'd hate to lose you as a friend even when the other didn't seem to work out."

"Come here, you." Amber stepped onto the porch and hugged him. Bo returned the hug, and she reached up and kissed him on the cheek. "Forgive me?"

Holding her felt good. Not an ounce of resentment or regret anywhere. "Of course. And one more thing."

"What?"

He tucked his face toward her ear. "Don't you buy his line about the milk delivery. He's had those goats for weeks."

"I knew it." She smiled up at him with a wicked glint in her eyes.

"Yes, ma'am, you certainly did." He kissed the top of her head. "I'll see about that corn. Y'all have a good evening." He turned away and charged down the steps. He'd have to go by the house and get his phone and see if his mama was speaking to him yet.

When he drove out to the house, MayLynn's car wasn't in the garage. Where was she keeping herself? Bo looked in the living room and kitchen for his phone, and then he checked the sitting room.

Bo traversed the stairs and entered his bedroom. No cell phone. Where would she have put his phone?

And where was she anyway?

****

MayLynn Anderson's heels clicked across the tiled floor of the attorney's business foyer. Emily Jackson led her into her office. "Have a seat, Mrs. Anderson. May I offer you some water or coffee?"

"No, dear. Thank you for meeting with me so late in the day."

Emily nodded and settled on her chair behind her desk. "I'm sorry I couldn't work you in earlier. I had a full schedule this afternoon."

"It's all right. I appreciate you were willing to stay open late to accommodate me."

"So what can I do for you?"

MayLynn placed her purse on the floor next to her chair. "Bo told me you were trying to get in touch with him. He was rather busy today, so I came instead."

"All right."

"Really. Since the land is in my name. I should be the one to deal with this anyway."

"That is true. However, the corporation is in Bo's name."

"And the land is in mine until I pass away, that is, then it will go to Bo."

"Did Bo tell you why I asked him to come in?"

"I listened to the message myself. You said you had found a clause in the agreement between Isaiah Justice and my husband that might be a solution to this problem with the land."

"That's right." Emily looked at the open folder on the desk in front of her. She handed a document to MayLynn. "If Isaiah Justice and his family ever moved back and claimed the land, the contract becomes null and void. The percentage of profit from the crop yield ceases, and Anderson Farms once again becomes owner of the thousand acres which has been owned by Isaiah Justice and now his daughter, Laura Justice Stanford, these past thirty years."

MayLynn closed her eyes for a moment and heaved a breath. "What a relief to hear you say that."

"It's a rather odd agreement," Emily stated gazing at the other woman.

"I don't know what you mean."

"Why give someone land—"

"It wasn't given to Isaiah. It was sold to him," MayLynn snapped.

Emily moved her head in a gesture of deferment. "Technically, yes. But for a mere pittance of what the land was worth. What I can't figure out is why sell someone land for practically nothing then make part of the contract that the buyer can't actually live on the land."

MayLynn didn't reply.

"You're the only person still alive who might know the answer to that question."

"I don't know why Zachary would have sold some of his family's farm. His father would have rolled over in his grave if he had known. But at least he had the sense enough to put that stipulation in because Laura Justice does not belong here, and obviously Zachary knew it might…be a problem at some point, so he made sure if that greedy family wanted their money, they had to stay away."

"This contract is only good for five more years. Then the land reverts to you anyway for one thousand dollars. It's the strangest contract I've ever run across."

"I know you will do what you can to protect the

interests of the Anderson family."

"I have to admit I'm really surprised at Martin Steen's incompetency. He should have spotted this right away. I can't wait to see his face when the sheriff serves the eviction papers on his clients. If he was really the best lawyer in town, he would have read the entire contract." Emily's face shone with pride.

"When can you start the eviction proceedings?"

"According to the contract, they have to establish intent to become residents."

"They've been living in that house for weeks now."

"Yeah, but that could mean Laura is just visiting. If she registers to vote or tries to get a driver's license or gets a utility bill in her—"

"Utility bill?"

"Yes. If she opens a utility account in her name at that address or, really, anywhere on the thousand acres, then she has violated the contract and loses the land."

"Are you sure? It applies to her too? Not just Isaiah?"

"Well." Emily shrugged. "The way the contract reads, it says the present owner for a term of thirty-five years. You might could make a case for it, I suppose, but since Isaiah isn't named specifically in the wording, just *present owner*, then I don't think it matters whether it was he or his daughter. And it might be that if Isaiah had sold his rights during that thirty-five years—which was his option to do as long as the land was not developed—then any owner who tried to squat on the land would make it so the land reverted to you."

"This is good. So, you just have to show they are planning on staying. And since the electric company is working on getting the power on there, Laura Stanford has probably already established residency."

"I'll see what I can find out."

"Thank you, Emily. You're very good at what you do."

Emily smiled. "I don't expect this will take me long."

****

Jane shut the door and walked to the house. She left

the basket of flowers on the porch, but brought the vases inside. Laura was out of the bathroom and lying on the couch.

"Hi." Jane set the vases on the table. "You okay?"

"Yeah. You think we could run the generator so I can watch television?"

"We could try, I suppose. I don't know how many channels we'll get without a satellite or Internet hook-up." Jane went to turn on the generator. She connected the plug of the television, and in a few minutes, they were sitting side-by-side watching the public television station.

"How about that?" Jane said, gesturing toward the door. "Did you see Bo brought us an air conditioner?"

"Oh?" She raised up, turning her head where Jane had indicated. "That's good."

"Want me to see if I can set it up?"

"Not right now." Her tone was flat when she spoke.

Jane looked at her mother-in-law closely. Laura's color was off. Jane reached forward and felt her cheek. "Are you sure you feel okay?"

"Quit hovering. I'd let you know if I didn't feel good."

"No, you wouldn't."

"If I felt like complaining, I would." She rested her head against the couch, not even looking at Jane when she spoke.

"Tomorrow's Sunday. Why don't we go to church? Did you go to church when you were living here?"

"Yes. It was mandatory."

"Mandatory?"

"Oh, yes. Everybody went to church. And in the summer time, the different churches would take turns having vacation Bible school. We'd be with the Baptists one week and the Methodists the next week and the Presbyterians the week after that and the Church of Christ after that. And by the time all the churches had their turn, it was time to go back to school."

"It was sort of like daycare for all the kids."

"Yes, it was. That's what I liked about Haven. The

town always took care of its own." Laura patted her hand. "I want this to be your hometown, Jane, so that you will be taken care of too."

Jane didn't like how this conversation was heading. "I don't need anyone to take care of me. I have you."

"Everybody needs someone to take care of them."

"Right. And we have each other," Jane reiterated.

"Well, yes," Laura said. "But I'm getting older, and I don't want you to be alone."

"Oh, come on. You're not going to get on that kick again of trying to set me up, are you?"

"Why don't you go after Bo Anderson?"

Jane laughed. "Go after Bo Anderson? Like I'm a hunter and he's the prey."

"He seems like a sweet boy, and he's mighty good looking." An expression that may have been longing entered Laura's eyes. "He looks so much like his daddy, I nearly get fluttery in the chest when I look at him."

"Is that why Bo's mom doesn't like you? Did you have a crush on his dad?"

Laura moved her head in a shrug that wasn't really a denial. "Zachary Anderson and I were best friends growing up. He was like the older brother I never had, but, no, we never dated. You couldn't convince MayLynn of that though. She was jealous of my friendship with Zachary. But, oh, he was so in love with that woman. He never had eyes for anyone else but her. She had a real bad temper, so he'd come out here for a visit while she cooled off and that would just make her even madder."

MayLynn's feelings made a lot of sense now. "How come your family moved away?"

Laura raised her hand in a dismissive gesture. "That was all a very long time ago."

"Is that your way of telling me you're not going to tell me?"

Laura stared at Jane for a moment, a gamut of emotions running across her face. "I don't know this for a fact, but I always suspected that MayLynn had an affair with my father."

Chapter Nine

Jane sat back as if the other woman had slapped her. "You're kidding."

Laura shrugged.

"Really? Why do you think your father had an affair with MayLynn?"

"I had gone away to college, and one Friday afternoon Zachary showed up on campus. He said he was in town for some business and did I want a ride home for the weekend, so he brought me home. My mother had died that spring, and when we pulled up to the house, there was MayLynn's car." Laura's face wore a far off expression, as if the memories were playing in her mind. As she spoke, a wistfulness entered her voice, so compelling a lump rose in Jane's throat. "Zachary and I sat in his truck for a few minutes, and he just stared at the house. Then he turned to me and said, 'Hey, let's go into town and get something to eat.' So we did. While we were there, he asked me to call my dad and let him know I was on my way home. I called, and later when Zachary brought me home, MayLynn's car was gone."

"What makes you think they were having an affair?"

Laura didn't answer for a moment. Jane thought perhaps she wasn't going to answer at all, but she turned and watched Jane soberly. "Because my dad lied to me and told me he'd been alone all evening. A few months after that, Dad moved up to Linten City. I was upset about it because I loved Haven, but he said, 'Don't worry, Laura, we still have our house there and we got a little money coming in from the crops. As long as we remember to pay our land taxes, we're set.' But, you know, we never came back here, and any time I talked about coming back—even for a visit—" She pinched her lips together. "He said no.

Soon after that, I met Mandy's dad, and he and I got married and went on to graduate school. And the rest, as they say, is history."

"So there was some agreement between your dad and Bo's dad about the crops. You all were getting some profit from the farming."

"I suppose. The money was direct deposited into Daddy's bank account once a year, and that's what I've always used to pay the taxes."

There were still missing pieces to this puzzle. "But who's been paying you all these years? Bo swears he didn't know anything about it."

Laura shrugged. "I don't know. You know I'm not good with details like that."

"It seems since you're a scientist, it would occur to you to be curious as to how your land was doing all this time and who's been paying you."

"I'm a scientist, yes, but not a farmer. I assumed it was Zachary Anderson all this time. I didn't know he had died or that he had a son."

"Bo was born after you left?"

"He must have been."

"Wow. It's hard to believe that your dad could have had an affair with Bo's mom. It sure would explain why she wasn't around when we ate supper the other night."

"She never liked me. Like I said, she was always so jealous though she never had a reason to be."

"I wonder if she loved your dad."

"Whether she did or didn't, she decided to stay with Zachary. She would have been crazy to leave him for my dad who barely had two pennies to rub together—and a man old enough to be her father, to boot. Anyway, all of that is water under the bridge, as far as I'm concerned. Only three people really know what took place back then, and two of them are dead now. There's no sense in me bringing it up."

"MayLynn would probably be relieved to know that."

"Oh, I don't know why she'd even care about

something that happened so long ago, unless she really wants to hold a grudge for that long. And if she does, well, I feel sorry for her."

Jane felt sorry for her too, if she was still jealous of Laura after all of these years.

"Where's your brush?" Laura asked.

"My brush?" Jane looked at the older woman. "It's in my room."

"Go get it, and I'll brush your hair."

Jane blinked. "Why do you want to brush my hair?"

"My mother used to do it for me right here in this very room. Let me do it for you."

"Okay, but I'm wondering what you did with the real Laura, who rarely noticed when her own hair needed brushing."

"Look. I had more important things to do in Linten City. Quit giving me a hard time and go get your brush."

Jane retrieved the brush and handed it to Laura before sitting down next to her on the couch.

"Take down your ponytail. I don't know why you have to wear it back most of the time. It's much prettier down."

Jane did so and turned her back to Laura. "Because it's hot here. Really hot, like sticky, muggy hot."

"Now that Bo has brought us an air conditioner, we don't have to be hot in here. Although, I must admit I do like listening to the crickets and the peepers at night." Laura smoothed Jane's black hair down her back with her hand then began to run the brush through it.

"The what?"

"The peep frogs." Laura's tone expressed exasperation.

Jane had heard them. "Those are frogs?"

"Yes, and be glad you hear them too because they keep the mosquito population contained."

"Somewhat. I've been bitten several times since we've been here. I hate those bloodsuckers."

"Well, what do you expect walking around before dawn? Mosquitoes come out at night." She spoke in a chastising tone.

A suspicion nipped at her. "Laura?"

"Yes?"

"Has it occurred to you that Bo could be your half-brother?"

Laura laughed. "No. I don't think so. He looks too much like Zachary."

"But he's got the same color hair as Mandy."

Laura didn't speak. Jane wondered if she was considering Jane's question. "I don't think so. Mandy has my hair color. MayLynn's hair was that color too, when she was younger," she said finally. She brushed a few more strokes then she paused. "But if he were, he would probably have a birthmark on his foot. My dad had it, I have it, and Mandy had it." Laura had her leg tucked under her, but she moved and tented her leg, showing Jane the small raspberry mark near her big toe. "Daddy said it was a Justice trait."

Jane remembered the mark on Mandy's foot.

"But whether Bo has the mark or not, he's not a Justice. He's an Anderson. My Lord, if it comes out that he's a bastard, MayLynn's liable to lose her mind, and she doesn't have far to go, unless she's changed an awful lot since we moved away." Laura resumed with the brush strokes. "And anyway, who's to say that if he is biologically my half-brother that he doesn't already know? I've never seen anybody so bent on helping people who have just come in and claimed property he didn't know wasn't his."

"I think he's just a very nice person, Laura."

"I have to admit his dad was that way too. His actual dad, not this little soap opera you've cooked up in your head."

****

Bo sat kicked back in his recliner watching television when he heard the front door open. In a few minutes, his mother walked into the living room. She wore a skirt and nice shoes.

Bo reached down to the side of the chair and moved the lever to bring down the footrest. "Hi," he said.

"Where've you been?"

"I had some business to attend to."

MayLynn's gaze fell to the dishes sitting on the end table next to him. Her lips thinned. "You couldn't wait until I got home to prepare supper?"

Bo shrugged. "I didn't know where you were, and I didn't have my cell phone to call you. Amber said she gave it to you at the diner."

MayLynn opened her purse and looked inside. Placing her hand there, she retrieved his cell phone, and walking over, handed it to him. "We do have a land line that you could have used."

Bo turned it on and checked. That was odd. He didn't have any messages—not even the one he had heard Jane leave him earlier in the day.

"I will thank you not to eat in here. We have a table in the kitchen and another one in the dining room."

Bo stood and collected his dishes. "I don't leave dirty dishes all over the place." He began to walk out of the room and toward the kitchen.

His mother followed him. "This is my house, and I want you to eat at the table."

Bo didn't answer. He went to the sink and turned on the faucet, intent on washing his own dirty dishes.

"Just leave those. I can do that."

"I know you can."

"Then leave them."

"Are you mad because I ate before you got home? I was hungry, Mom." He took a sponge, squirted it with some dish soap, and cleaned the plate.

"Bo!"

Bo turned his head toward the woman standing on the other side of the kitchen. "Leave the dishes."

Bo turned off the faucet. He picked up a dish towel and dried his hands. Going to the back door, he stuck his socked feet in his boots. "I'll be out at the barn if you need me."

****

That night Jane couldn't sleep. She decided to take a walk and soon she was at Hesed rock. Bo's truck was at the barn, but the windows in the apartment were dark. Jane bypassed the building and lay back on the rock, looking up at the nighttime sky. She remembered MayLynn's face as she stood in her garden and showed Jane her flowers. Even though she was in her fifties, she was still a beautiful woman. Jane could see how Laura's dad could fall in love with MayLynn, as young as she was back then, and if he was grieving his wife, perhaps MayLynn's youth and beauty appealed to him.

Certainly, Bo couldn't have known about the affair, if there had been one, since he hadn't even been born yet. And if MayLynn hadn't disclosed her feelings to him, then he certainly was in the dark about why she didn't like Laura—and it wasn't Jane's place to tell him anything.

As Laura had said, it was all a very long time ago. And best if any skeletons stayed in the closets where they'd been stored for many years.

"O Jane, Jane. Wherefore art thou, Jane?"

At the sound of Bo's voice, Jane sat up and turned toward the balcony where Bo was standing. His clever quotation from Shakespeare brought a lump in her throat.

"More Romeo and Juliet. Do you talk this way to Amber?" she called up to him.

"She speaks. O, speak again, bright angel." Bo raised his arm dramatically. "For thou art As glorious to this night, being o'er my head, As is a winged messenger of heaven. Unto the white, upturned, wondering eyes Of mortals that fall back to gaze on him When he bestrides the lazy-puffing clouds And sails upon the bosom of the air."

"Does he really say bosom of the air?"

He paused before speaking. "Yes, he really does."

"And she still went out with him?"

Bo chuckled. "They were both very young. It didn't turn out well for them."

"Mainly because their families couldn't get along." Jane wondered if perhaps the feuding Montagues and Capulets stemmed from a broken heart from a previous generation. "What are you doing out here?"

"Enjoying my space. Let me get my shoes on, and I'll come down there."

The need to know whether he truly was an Anderson—or not—kindled and burst into flame. "Don't put on your shoes."

"Why not?"

"I've taken mine off." Jane lifted up one foot. "See?"

"Your feet are a lot prettier than mine."

"Just come on down here, and let me decide."

"I need my shoes on. What if I step on a rock or a sharp stick?"

The flame faltered. *It's not my business. It all happened a long time ago.* "You have tender feet. I'll have to remember that."

"Want a beer?" he asked.

"Sure."

In a few moments, Bo came downstairs and settled next to her on the rock. He handed her one of the beer bottles he held in his hand.

"Thanks." She twisted the top off. Bo held his bottle to hers and clinked the glass.

"Cheers," he said and took a drink.

"What are we drinking to?" she asked before bringing her bottle to her lips and drinking. The drink was cold and felt good going down her throat.

"To the milkman."

"The milkman. What does that mean?"

"It means Amber has given up on me and is now keeping company with Richard Cron who milks his own cows and goats and makes house calls to deliver the milk."

"Oh. I'm sorry." Even though she had to bite her lip from smiling.

Bo didn't hide his own smile. Even his eyes crinkled as he gazed at her. "Don't be. We parted friends, and that was what I was hoping for."

"You saw this coming?"

Bo stared off into the night. His face took on a reflective expression. "Yeah. I think we both did. I haven't been in love with her for a long time. We had become good friends, though neither of us admitted it until today. She has had her eye on Richard, apparently. And, me? Well, I haven't been able to quit thinking about...."

"About what?"

Bo smiled. He reached over and patted the top of her hand. "About being a good neighbor."

Chapter Ten

Ribbons of hope and fear spiraled in Jane's chest. Was he saying he was attracted to her? Or did he mean she and Laura moving in had occupied too much of his time lately? Perhaps the hand pat was to soften the blow.

"It was something Amber and I should have dealt with months ago, but we didn't. I think because we were worried about losing each other as friends."

"It's good to have friends."

"I agree."

"So, what now?"

Bo lay back on his elbows. Jane watched his long legs and his boots as he crossed his ankles. "I have a great big party."

"You're going to throw yourself a break-up party?"

"No. I need to start planning my beginning of the harvest party. It's an annual tradition. We have migrant workers who will be coming in, and we have a big barbecue the first night. Then the next day we work like dogs until all the beans and the rest of the crops are in." He turned to her. "I'm afraid I won't get to see you very much after we start harvest. It's grueling, but that's what this whole year has been about—getting us to the harvest. I sure wouldn't mind one more good rain though. The soil is mighty dry."

"Maybe you could pray for rain."

"Are you a praying woman?"

"Yes, of course I am."

"Maybe you could pray for rain then. Put in a good word for me."

"Don't you pray, Bo?"

"It says in the Bible the rain falls on the just and the unjust, so I never could bring myself to pray for rain."

"I don't think it literally meant rain."

"My dad used to pray for rain. If ever we were going through a dry spell, each night at supper when he'd say grace, he'd ask God to make it rain. And sometimes it would, but sometimes it wouldn't. I've never seen a connection between prayer and the weather because after my dad was gone and no one at our table prayed for rain, it still rained, you know?"

"Maybe prayer is so when God does intervene, we will notice it."

Bo studied her face. He reached forward and swept her hair over her shoulder. "It's hard to imagine you could still believe in God when you've had so much tragedy in your life."

"It's because of the tragedy that I know God is with me. I couldn't have survived if I didn't believe there had to be some reason for all of it."

"What could possibly be the reason?"

"I don't know. Maybe I'll never know. But God does know, and that's a comfort."

Bo cupped her cheek. He leaned toward her. "I want to kiss you, but I'm not thinking too clear because I've had several beers tonight."

"Yeah, I thought maybe you had been drinking when you compared me to an angel."

"You *are* an angel." His hand had moved to cup her neck, and it felt warm against her skin.

Jane shook her head. "I think you're the angel."

Bo leaned back with an amused laugh. "Me?"

"Because you've been so good to Laura and me when you didn't have to be."

"I couldn't help but be good to a dark-haired angel who basked on the rock in the soft dawn light," he whispered. His face inched closer to hers. Jane closed her eyes.

Jane's heart sped up. *He's going to kiss me.* She was torn between wanting him to and wanting to turn away. *I'm not ready for this. Is he ready for this? He just broke up with his girlfriend. This is wrong, isn't it?*

Bo placed a chaste kiss on her cheek. Then he lay his whiskered face next to hers for a moment.

Jane tensed, knowing he was going to kiss her on the lips. *What will I do? Let him?* Jane waited. She realized she'd been holding her breath. She opened her mouth, willing herself to exhale, inhale.

Bo is a kind man. Mandy is gone. I'm not being unfaithful. Mandy would like Bo. He'd like him because Bo has taken care of his mother.

Jane reached out her arm and snaked her hand around his side. She felt the breadth of his frame, the firm muscles beneath the texture of his shirt.

"Are you okay?" he whispered next to her ear.

The tender concern in his voice filled her heart. She bowed her head and tucked it into the front of his shirt. His arms went around her, and he held her.

I think I'm okay. I'm scared, but I think I'm okay.

But she couldn't say the words. She could only think them, but Bo's warm hand patting her back made her think that he understood. Jane relaxed into him, closing her eyes.

And she prayed for rain.

****

Jane and Laura were painting the walls of the kitchen when a knock sounded on the door. Laura didn't pause in her work, so Jane carefully placed the roller in the pan and answered the summons.

Miles stood on the porch. "Hi. I brought some windows out to replace the broken ones."

"I thought you were going to finish the floor today."

He nodded. "That was my plan, but if it rains, I'd really like to get the two windows in that are completely busted out—the one in your bedroom and the bathroom."

Could it be true? Jane looked up at the sky. She saw a few scattered clouds.

"Do you think it's going to rain?" she asked.

"It's always going to rain." Miles smiled widely. "I'm in construction. I have to plan for the rain."

Jane returned his smile and went back to the kitchen. She picked up her roller. "Thank you for thinking of the windows."

Last night soon after their conversation of prayer, rain, and breaking up with Amber, Bo had walked her home. Miles had placed a utility light on the porch, and in its illumination, Bo's eyes had sparkled with hunger. Jane thought he might kiss her again, on the mouth this time, but he hadn't. He hadn't even come on the porch, just stood on the stairs with his hand on the tree.

"Good night, Jane," he'd said.

"Good night," she'd responded. She waited a second or two, but he didn't move. She realized he was waiting for her to go inside before he left.

Jane entered the house. She turned the key on the deadbolt Miles had installed. And in the quiet of the night, she head Bo's footsteps leave the stairs.

"Jane?" Miles' voice brought her back to the present. He carried a window through the house and went into her bedroom then came back out.

"I called the electric company yesterday to get y'all some bulbs. They have a program where they give customers so many LED bulbs to encourage them to use them. I thought I could get yours and bring them to you today."

"That sounds great."

"Well, except they couldn't find you in their files. I got them to look under yours and Laura's names. Don't you have an account with them?"

"To tell you the truth, maybe we don't. We never formally went down there and opened one."

"Huh. Maybe Bo added the house to his account. Your house ain't that far from his barn anyway."

"He was the one that got the electrician out here."

"Yeah, and he was the one who called me too. He sure is a good neighbor."

Jane nodded, affection warming her heart. "Yes. Yes, he is."

Miles left the room, and soon she could hear sounds of him pulling the old pane from the wall.

"We can't let Bo pay for our electricity," Jane said.

"No. That wouldn't be right," Laura returned.

"I'll talk to him and find out if he put it in his name, or if Harvey, the electrician, is just doing the work with the understanding that we would go to the electric company and establish an account."

"I wouldn't think they'd do anything without money passing hands."

"That's probably true. If Bo has paid for us to get the electricity, then we need to pay him back."

"I agree. That boy has gone way beyond the decent thing to do and is qualifying for sainthood. I'm telling you, he is Zachary Anderson all over again."

Jane smiled. She hoped Laura was right—that Bo was exactly like his father—and that his father was Zachary Anderson.

"I guess you need to go to the power company and open the account."

"Me? This is your house."

Laura didn't look away from her painting. "Look, girl. You know I'm not good at all of this stuff like paying bills and making sure there is food in the house. It makes sense for you to take care of it, like you did in Linten City."

"You say that but, apparently, you didn't have any problem paying the taxes every single year without saying one word to me about it."

"My daddy always said, 'Land means everything.' No matter what, I had to be sure we didn't lose it. The taxes had to be paid."

"Did Philip and Mandy know about all of this?"

"Philip did. He'd remind me when it was time to pay the taxes, and a few times we talked about using some of the money from the account to buy something, like the down payment on the house, but we never did."

"Why didn't you?"

"I don't know. I guess we thought we might need it for

a rainy day."

"Your house burning down and losing your husband and son wasn't a rainy day?"

"No. That was more of a tsunami. No amount of money was going to fix it. Do you concur?"

Jane hummed an agreement.

****

Jane and Laura sat in the same booth they had occupied the first time they'd eaten here when MayLynn Anderson had choked. Jane's eyes had scanned the restaurant when they first came in, but Jane only recognized Amber.

The restaurant was busy—no vacant tables or stools at the counter and a charter bus took up half the parking lot. Amber flitted from one table to the next like a humming bird to too many flowers, and she was doing a pretty good job, but Jane knew she could use some help. They'd been there twenty minutes without even getting a menu yet.

Jane slid across the bench.

"Where are you going?"

"Where do you think? She needs some help."

"I thought she was competition."

Jane wrinkled her nose in disapproval. "He's not a dog bone."

Laura smirked. Jane walked away before she could reply.

Jane approached Amber who had a tray full of large plastic tumblers of iced drinks. She held out her hands. "Let me help."

Amber's tense expression eased a bit. She surrendered the tray. "Thanks. It goes to those two tables there." She motioned to two booths on the other side of the room. Jane held the tray and went to distribute the drinks. With the drinks doled out, she studied the faces of the people at one table. Menus sat open on the table.

"Are you guys ready to order?"

Heads nodded. Beginning with the woman closest to her on the left, Jane listened as each person stated what they wanted to eat. Then she moved to the next table.

"Great," she said. "I'll put your orders in." She walked behind the counter where Amber was putting ice in glasses. "Do you have an order pad?"

"Seriously? You're going to waitress?"

"I am a waitress, and I don't mind lending a hand."

"Thanks." She slapped a pad and pen on Jane's palm. Jane began writing on it. "What are you doing?"

"Writing down their orders."

"Whose orders?"

"The tables I just took the drinks to."

Amber turned her head in the direction of the tables. "There are twelve people over there."

"Yeah."

"You can remember twelve orders from memory," she said in disbelief.

"Not that hard. Four cheese burgers. Two club sandwiches—one hold the mayo. All with fries. One salad, three specials, a vegetable plate—fried okra, crowder peas, creamed corn, and collards, and another vegetable plate—creamed corn, cabbage, tomatoes, and hominy." Jane tore off the top paper and held it out to her. "Want me to clip it to the window?"

Amber's eyes widened. She nodded her head.

"Want me to work on those drinks?"

"Okay." Amber handed her the paper with the drink orders.

"What other tables need to order?"

"That whole section."

Jane looked at the tables. Six of them.

No sweat.

Two hours later, Jane had one knee propped on a bench seat while she wiped down a table.

"Hey," Amber said.

Jane straightened and looked over her shoulder. Amber gave her a tired smile. "I owe you. Because of your help, I was able to feed sixty people lunch and sell all of my sweet potato-pecan rolls."

She set some bills on the table. "Here are your tips plus an hourly wage."

Jane shook her head. "You don't have to pay me."

"You'll make me feel bad if you don't take it. Lord knows you earned it."

"I was glad to help."

"Listen. Friday is usually pretty busy around here. I sure wouldn't mind if you came and helped out. That way, I could do some baking as well."

"Yeah. I could probably do that, as long as we're here." Jane took a final swipe across the table.

Amber held out her hand for the cloth. "I'll take that."

"All right."

"I really appreciate what you did today." Amber's serious expression made Jane pause. "I didn't expect that."

"I don't know how to do a lot of things, but I know how to wait tables."

"You certainly do. How do you remember so many orders without writing them down?"

"Pneumonics."

"What?"

"Memory game. I lived in seven different foster homes when I was growing up. So, when somebody tells me what they want to eat. I put the food in a room in one of the houses I lived in, and it helps me remember what they ordered."

"Jane!" Laura yelled from the table where she had been sitting for a couple of hours now. "Are we going home any time soon?"

"Sure."

"Wait. You didn't get any lunch," Amber said.

"That's all right."

"No, it isn't. What do you want?"

Jane lifted her shoulders. "I don't know. The special looked good. Got any more chicken and dumplings?"

"Sure do."

"It's not made from that rooster of Bo's that doesn't know how to tell time, is it?"

Amber laughed. "You and MayLynn hate that chicken, don't you?"

****

Jane had gone into town to do laundry since they didn't have a washer or dryer. There was a Laundromat close to *The Bread Basket*, and even though Bo had the facilities to do laundry at his apartment, she didn't feel quite comfortable there since the bathtub incident.

As she drove up to the house, the police car made her heart stop. She parked and got out of the car. A sheriff was at the door with his hat in his hand. Laura stood talking to him, the sad expression on her face really troubled Jane.

What had happened? Jane hurried out of the car and onto the porch.

"I appreciate you, Caden. Thank you for coming out."

"I'm so sorry, Mrs. Stanford. Truly, I am."

"It's not your fault. I blame myself."

"Blame yourself?" Jane asked.

"Good day, ma'am." The man said nodding to her before returning the hat to his head and going down the porch stairs.

Laura walked inside the house but left the door ajar. Jane followed her inside. "What was that about? What's wrong?"

"We've lost it. The house. The land. It no longer belongs to me."

"What? Why?"

"The Andersons have evicted us. We have to leave."

"Bo wouldn't do that. You've got to be mistaken."

Laura picked up several papers she had laid on the table. "He did, but he had every right to. I didn't abide by the agreement."

She handed the papers to Jane, who looked at a section circled in yellow highlighter.

During the said time of this agreement, the owner is not to live or occupy any part of the land herein. If the owner does occupy the land or any buildings herein and establishes residency, then the owner gives up the rights to said property and the land reverts to the Anderson family and no more profits will be paid to the owner. This contract will be null and void.

"But, you didn't know about this, did you?"

"No, I didn't, but I should have."

"But what about Mr. Steen? Let's call him."

"He's already been out here. He said we could appeal it, but in the meantime, we'd have to vacate the premises.

"I don't understand. Why doesn't Bo just disregard the agreement? He's let us live here. He's helped us get settled in the house. Why would he turn around and want us out?"

"Martin said he'd decided this was best, what with all of the money that the farm had lost on paying me every year. Apparently, he's planted some high cash crops on our land that the agreement says we get a percentage of."

"Well, we don't care about that as long as you can live in the house."

"I guess he thinks we do."

"I can't believe it. He's been so nice."

"He is nice. This isn't his fault. It's mine. My dad told me lots of times, the value of that land is lost if I ever went back. I thought he just meant that it would never feel like home again. He was wrong about that. I've been happier here than I've felt in a long time. But really, he wasn't wrong about it, because what he meant was I really couldn't ever go back. I was stupid, Jane, and I'm sorry."

"We're not giving up. I'm going to talk to Bo."

"Just leave it be. It was silly to come here in the first place. You were right. Just to drop everything, to leave our lives in Linten City—that wasn't the right thing to do."

"Maybe it was the right thing to do."

Laura held Jane's face. "You are so good to me. Always supportive. I couldn't have had a better daughter if I had given birth to you myself." She stepped back. "We've got three days."

"We have to be out in three days?"

"Yes." Laura sighed. "I wish I had listened to my father. He tried to tell me I could never come back." She walked across the room to the doorway of her bedroom.

"I'm going to lie down for a little while. Do you mind?"

"No. Of course not."

Anger burned in Jane. *Why?* Why had Bo acted as if he wanted them there then had just gone behind their backs, making arrangements to have them booted out as soon as they unknowingly broke the contract? Could he really be so two-faced? Maybe he really was Laura's half-brother. If he was, then she'd have every right to stay on the land, to stay in this house.

She got into the car and drove up to the barn. No truck. Turning the car around, she headed to his house, went to the garage, and didn't see his truck there either. She pulled out her phone and dialed his number.

"Hi," he answered.

"It's Jane," she said tersely.

"Yeah, I know. Is everything all right?"

She snorted. "You're kidding, right? We've just been evicted. No, we're not all right. Why did you lie to me? Why did you help us get the house all fixed up if you were just—?"

"Hold it. Hold it. Hold it. Jane!" Bo began talking over her until she finally paused. "What do you mean you've been evicted?"

"The sheriff just came out and served papers. We broke the contract. Why didn't you say anything about our being here violating it? If you had just given us some warning—we don't care about what you grow on the land. Laura doesn't care about the money or what you grow. She only cares about the house, and I only care that she's happy. Why did you do this?"

"I don't know that I did anything. Where are you right now?"

"I'm at your house, but I'm going back to…what I thought was our house. We've got three days to vacate."

"Don't move. I'll sort this out."

"I've got to get back to Laura."

"Okay. Just promise me, you won't leave your house until we talk. And it is your house, Jane. Yours and Laura's.

No one's taking it from you."

"It's already done, Bo." Jane pressed the end button on the cell phone. She placed it next to her on the seat and drove back to the house to begin to pack the few belongings they had.

Chapter Eleven

What is going on? What was Jane talking about?

Bo had put the tractor in neutral when Jane called him. He shut off the engine, and signaled to Jonathan in the other tractor to keep going.

Going through his contacts on his cell phone, Bo found and dialed Emily's number. When she answered, he didn't even bother identifying himself.

"What is going on?"

"What do you mean?"

"I just got a call from Jane Stanford saying I evicted her and Laura from their house."

There was silence for a few seconds. "You knew about this."

"Since when?"

"You and your mother—"

"My mother." Anger burned in Bo's chest, and he raised his voice. "My mother? Have you been meeting with my mother?"

"Well, yes. She's the owner of the property, after all."

"My God, what have you done, Emily?"

"I didn't do anything. All I had to do was wait. The contract states if they establish residence they break the contract, and they no longer have rights to the property."

"Why didn't you tell me this? You never said anything about it."

"It's a minor clause, buried in the contract. I didn't find it right away, but I did tell you. Or I tried to. I left you a message—"

"When?"

"Weeks ago. On your cell phone."

"And then what happened?"

"Your mother came in and handled it. As the owner of

the property, she has every right to anyway, Bo."

"How could you not let me know what was going on?" he snapped.

"I figured your mother was keeping you informed. This wasn't about the corporation. It was the land."

"They're nearly the same thing."

"Except that legally, they're not the same thing. You own the corporation of Anderson Farms, but your mother owns the land."

Bo ran a hand down his face in frustration. "You stop this."

"What do you mean?"

"They're not leaving. We're not evicting them. Whatever it takes, you undo what you've done."

"I can't. They broke the contract. It's done." She spoke in her efficient lawyer voice which grated on Bo's nerves.

"Then we'll give them the land."

"You really can't give them anything. It's not your land to give. I'm sorry."

"MayLynn will give them back the land, by God. Emily, you better help me make this right." Bo hung up the phone.

Jonathan had finished the row and came back up next to him. "What's wrong?"

"My mother." Bo shook his head. "I've got to go."

"All right. I'll finish up. Maybe get Sonya to drive. You okay with that?"

"Yeah. Whatever you think."

Bo walked into the house twenty minutes later. MayLynn was in the kitchen canning tomatoes. She looked up from the stove and wiped her hands on her apron.

By her stubborn expression, Bo knew she'd been expecting him to come in. She had anticipated this fight.

"Well?"

"Take off your shoes."

Bo arched an eyebrow at her. "Not this time."

"Don't test me."

"You're already testing me, Mom. Why?"

She turned back to her task, picking up the jar tongs. "Look. I didn't do anything. Why are you attacking me?"

"You erased messages on my cell phone. You met with Emily Jackson, and you kept it from me. I have done everything to make Laura and Jane feel welcome here, and in two weeks, you've destroyed all of the trust I've—"

"Why?" She screamed, her temper shooting up like fireworks on the Fourth of July. "Why would you go to all of that trouble for that...that tramp!"

Bo raised his hands in confusion. "What are you talking about?"

"That...that woman you think so much of. She had an affair with your father!"

Shock paralyzed Bo. "Laura?"

"Yes. Her."

Bo shook his head. "Is that what all of this has been about?"

MayLynn's fury shot forth from her eyes. "Yes, that's what this is about. She went after him, right in front of my face, and even when she went off to college, he'd go see her. She makes me sick."

Bo sat down at the table. This is what all of this was about? Dad had an affair with Laura?

"Dad? Are you sure they had an affair?"

"Yes, I'm sure."

"How? I mean, maybe they were just friends or something."

She made an ugly guttural sound of anger. "Don't you dare defend her. I know what they were doing."

"Well, okay." Bo didn't believe it, but his mother was convinced, and it was useless to argue with her about it. "So they had an affair. But Dad chose you. I mean, obviously, it didn't last. Right? And anyway, that was a long time ago."

"So typical. A man's answer. Big deal. An affair. Just sleep with whoever you want to, and it means nothing!" She turned off the stove and threw the jar tongs onto the counter.

"You know I'm not that way, and I don't think Dad was either. Mom, he loved you."

MayLynn crossed her arms and, turning aside her head, she stared at a spot on the wall.

"Mama, I want you to let them stay," Bo said calmly.

"No." The venom in her voice made the word seem almost like a growl.

"Yes."

"She is the one who screwed up." MayLynn pointed at the air in the direction of the little white shack two miles from the house. "She broke the contract. They were to never come back."

"Why not?"

MayLynn didn't answer.

I am going to get to the bottom of this if it's the last thing I do. "If Dad was having an affair with Laura, he wouldn't have put that in the contract. If he loved her, he would want her close. Was this because her dad found out they were having an affair?"

She shuddered.

Hmm. He was getting closer. "Did Isaiah Justice blackmail Dad?"

She looked at him with narrowed eyes. "Don't you..." Her breath hissed through her gritted teeth. "Don't you talk about Isaiah like that. He was...he was...I...I...." She covered her face with her hands and wailed a gut-wrenching cry before crumpling.

Bo charged across the kitchen and caught her before she hit the floor. "Mom! Mama!"

She cried as if her heart was breaking. Fear erupted in Bo. He'd seen his mother have a lot of hissy fits, but he'd never seen her fall completely apart like this. He held her to him, patting her shoulder.

"Mama, you're okay. You're going to be fine. Please."

Her weeping continued for a while, until she seemed to cry herself out. She sat up. Bo retrieved a tissue, and kneeling beside her, he handed it to her.

"It's okay, Mom."

"No. No, it's not okay," she said finally in a desperate voice. "You can't allow that woman to stay here."

"Whatever it is, just tell me." Bo looked at her, willed her to just tell him the damn truth, this secret that was eating her alive. "Whatever her dad did to you, Mom, he can't hurt you—"

She shook her head. "Oh, Bo. Isaiah would have never hurt me." A softness crept across her face. "He was very gentle."

Everything stilled. He studied his mother. "He was...what?"

MayLynn stared at the floor.

"Mom?"

She was the one who had an affair.

"I see." Bo breathed out the words. "So that was why Dad wanted him gone. Because he wanted to keep Isaiah Justice away from you. He gave him a quarter of the land with the promise that he'd never come back, and he paid him a percentage of our profits to be sure he kept that promise."

Bo stood up and walked to the Hoosier cabinet. "If Laura knows about this, she doesn't care. You are going to give her the land back. Do you understand?"

"I will not—"

"That's enough," he said sharply, maybe too sharply, but at this point, Bo didn't give a damn. "I want you to call Emily Jackson by four o'clock this afternoon and take care of this. If you don't fix this, I will leave this house right now, and you will not see me anymore unless it is about the farm."

"You don't mean that," she said brokenly.

There was a scratch on the top of the cabinet. It went straight through the paint to the wood. Bo watched his finger trace the mark. "Please don't make me prove it."

She took a shuddering breath. "I don't ever want this brought up again, Bo. Not ever."

That scratch had to be at least ten inches across. What had caused it? "I just have one more question."

"What?"

"Is Isaiah my biological father?"

MayLynn gasped. Then she began to weep again.

Oh, dear God.

Bo balled up his fist. He watched the veins on the back of his hand stand out from his skin. With effort, he uncurled his fingers and laid his palm flat on the wooden surface. He looked at the back door and through the window to the sunlit patio.

His rooster crowed once, then again. A third time, the bird made its call. Somebody really needed to teach that bird when daybreak was.

Bo strode to the door, opened it, and walked through. He shut the door quietly behind him and headed for the shed to get his hatchet.

****

A text came into Jane's phone from Bo. *Problem addressed. Land is Laura's. E Jackson should be contacting you soon. B.*

Huh. Well, maybe she had misjudged Bo. Maybe he really hadn't known what was going on.

She texted him back.

Thank you.

No reply.

Something prodded at Jane. An uneasiness. She called Bo's number, but he didn't pick up. Martin Steen called and informed them that MayLynn Anderson had had a change of heart and wanted to disregard the clause in the contract. As a matter of fact, she had offered to give them the land outright.

Wow. MayLynn had had a change of heart? MayLynn had offered to give them the land? Was she the one behind all of this?

Guilt tore at Jane. She had accused Bo of kicking them out when he hadn't had anything at all to do with it.

That night, she lay in bed unable to sleep. She'd attempted to call Bo twice more, but he hadn't picked up either time. Finally, she dressed with the intention of finding him. Laura was already in bed and the house dark. On the front porch, Jane slipped on her shoes and walked out to the barn, taking the chance he was there.

It was past midnight, much too late to pay a house call. But he might be awake.

Would he come out on the balcony again and greet her, as he had done before? What if he didn't see her out here? What if he did see but ignored her?

His text had been terse, and in their last conversation, she had accused him of lying to her and kicking them out of their house. He had a right to be angry, didn't he? Of course, she had a right to be angry, too, but she shouldn't have jumped to the conclusion he had anything to do with their eviction. Not when he had bent over backward to be sure they had what they needed for the house. Even though he had no idea Laura had even owned the land, he had made them feel welcome.

The need to settle this gnawed at her. She could knock on the door or she could use the key. Going into someone's abode in the middle of the night was probably a dumb thing to do in this part of the country. She was liable to get shot.

Did Bo have a gun?

This was dumb. He probably wasn't even there.

As she approached the barn, she saw his truck parked outside of it. She began to mount the stairs. About halfway up, her glance strayed to the rock, and she gasped.

Bo was lying unconscious on the rock, a liquor bottle clutched in his hand. Jane flew down the stairs. "Bo. Bo!" She climbed the rock and knelt beside him. Relief poured over her when she saw he was breathing. "Bo?"

Nothing.

She patted his cheek a few times. "Bo, honey, wake up."

His eyes fluttered open, and he smiled. Then he closed them again.

"Bo." She slapped his cheek harder this time.

He flinched away from her. "Ow." He blinked at her.

"Oh. It's you."

"Can you sit up?"

"I can try." He struggled a little bit. Jane put her arm behind his shoulders and pulled. Bo lifted the bottle to his face. "I think I figured out the problem."

"Here we go," Jane said when he was in a sitting position.

He indicated the bottle. "This isn't the problem."

"It isn't, huh?"

"No. It's the...the—"

A low rumble sounded in the distance.

Thunder.

If she didn't get him inside, they were going to get struck by lightning.

"Did you hear that?"

"Yes." Jane scooted to the edge of the rock. "Come on. Let's get in your apartment."

"It sounded like thunder. Do you think it's going to rain, Jane? Hey, I made a rhyme."

"Yes, you're very talented."

"No, you're talented. Your praying is working. I can smell the rain coming. Can you?"

Jane sniffed. All she could smell was whiskey. "Come on, Bo. Let's...."

The bottle turned over and liquid spilled on the rock. "Oops." He began to laugh. "You know what my buddy, Jonathan, calls that? Alcohol abuse."

Jane jumped from the rock and pulled him with her. "Funny. Come on before you get booze all over you. I hope you can stand up."

"Of course, I can stand up." He slid down the edge of the rock, and his boots hit the ground. "See?"

"You're leaning against the rock."

"All right."

Jane sidled up next to him and put her arm around his waist. He put his arm around her shoulders. "This is nice. You fit real nice next to me."

"Yes. Very nice. Let's go." She took a step then

another one. He walked with her.

"Where are we going?"

"To your apartment."

"My apartment. I do my own laundry there."

"That's good."

"I can cook. Really well. You know I make the best barbecue in the entire county. I make it for the Harvest party. You can come to the party. You will come, won't you?"

"Yes, I'll come to the party." They were at the bottom of the stairs. Jane put her foot on the bottom stair. "Here we go. Up. Up. Up."

"Up, up, up," he repeated.

On the balcony, he put his hand on the rail. "It's a nice view up here. O Romeo, Romeo. Wherefore art thou, Romeo? Deny…" He sighed and leaned heavily on the rail, wrenching Jane down with him. Their bodies were angled out over the driveway below. "Deny my father and refuse my name." Jane pushed him upward and back so they wouldn't tumble over the rail. He raised his voice and gripped Jane's sleeve. "Or, if thou wilt not, be but my sworn love."

"Easy, Bo."

"And I'll no longer be a…an Anderson."

"A Capulet, isn't it?"

He snorted. "No. I'm pretty sure it's be but my sworn love, and I'll no longer be an Anderson."

They were to the door now. It was partially open. Jane walked him inside.

"I've got to sit down. I'm tired," Bo's voice slurred a bit as he spoke.

"We're almost there."

He headed for the couch, and Jane let him lead them. "I've had a really hard day," he said vehemently.

"I know."

He collapsed on the couch, and with Jane under his arm, she fell with him. Immediately, he was still.

"Bo?"

He didn't respond.

Jane shimmied out from under him. His eyes were closed. She shook her head and bent over, picked up his legs, and settled him into a lying position. He shifted onto his side. Jane retrieved his comforter from his bed and covered him with it. She gazed at him for a moment then she went down to Hesed Rock, took the bottle, poured the rest of the whiskey onto the ground, and dropped the empty container in the garbage can in Bo's kitchen. She turned out the lights, locked the door, and walked home. Their talk would have to wait another day.

Lightning lit up the sky, and Jane hoped she could get home before it started to rain. The thunder sounded a few seconds later. Once she was at the house, she entered. Laura had left a lamp on in the corner, and the air conditioner kept the oppressive heat outside of the house. It certainly was nice to have electricity. For the second time that night, Jane went to bed. She must have fallen asleep because a horrible sound wrenched her out of sleep.

What was that? It sounded as if a train was running across the roof!

Jane ran to Laura's bedroom and shook the older woman. "Laura. Laura! We have to get out of here. I think the roof is coming off the house."

Laura sat up and rubbed her eyes. "What?"

"The roof. Something's wrong. We need to get out of the house."

Laura smiled. "Oh, don't be silly. That's just rain on the tin roof, Jane."

"Are you sure?"

"Sure, I'm sure. I heard that sound every time we had a rainstorm growing up. It's fine. Go back to sleep."

"Sleep? How can I sleep with all that noise?"

"That's the sound of crops growing. There's no sound better than that."

"Except you're not a farmer."

"No. But I grew up the daughter of a farmhand. That sound meant he had work, and we had food to eat. Now go back to bed."

Go back to bed. With that metallic cacophony above her head?

****

A few days went by. Jane didn't hear from Bo. She thought perhaps he needed some space, so she decided to give it to him. Amber called Jane and asked her to come in for the breakfast shift. Cathy, Amber's regular waitress was home with two sick kids, and Amber had agreed to make homemade bread for a fundraising auction in a nearby town. If Jane could come in and lend a hand, Amber could get the bread made without any inconvenience with the regular breakfast patrons.

It wasn't dawn yet, when headlights shone through the plate glass window. Jane turned from the coffee maker, and saw Bo's truck illuminated by the parking lot light. The door opened, and he walked to the back of the truck then came into the door of the restaurant.

He didn't meet her eyes when he spoke. "Hi." Carrying a basket of greens, he took it back to the kitchen. "Heard you were helping Amber out."

"She sure is," Amber said without leaving her post at the counter.

"Need a hand?" Jane said, glad to see Bo and following him out of the diner even before he answered.

"I can manage," he said on the way to the truck. "It's just some tomatoes, pecans, and half-runner beans."

"I don't mind. I've been wanting to talk to you." The door shut behind her, and Bo paused at the lowered tailgate of his truck.

He looked at her for the first time. "About what?"

Bo's eyes were so blue as he gazed at her that Jane blinked.

"About you straightening out the contract we broke by coming here. About me apologizing for accusing you of something you didn't do. Things like that."

Jane examined Bo's face. Fatigue lined those eyes. Was sorting out the land issue the cause of his stress, was more

144

rain needed for the crops, or was it the upcoming harvest?

He shook his head. "It's fine. I'm glad it worked out."

"Is something…is it something else? The other night when I came by your apartment, I was worried about you."

He shifted a boot, and it made a scraping sound against the gravel. "Was I there?"

"Yes. You don't remember?"

He pursed his lips. "What did I do? Do I want to know?"

"You were asleep on the rock. I made sure you got inside the apartment okay."

"Thanks. How late was it?"

"Midnight or so."

He made an irritated sound. "I wish you wouldn't walk over kingdom come in the dark of night. It worries me."

"I was okay, and anyway, you would have gotten caught in the rain if I hadn't come along."

"It would have served me right. I usually don't drink like that. It was stupid."

"We all do dumb things at times."

"I suppose. Did you make it home before the rain?"

"Yes."

"You should have stayed."

"It seems an invasion of privacy to be in someone's apartment when they're asleep."

"Passed out, you mean. You probably owe me one after I walked in on you in the bathroom."

"I think it bothered you more than it bothered me."

"It didn't bother me." He reached down and picked up a box of tomatoes.

"Scared you." She bit her lip to keep from smiling.

He set the box down on the tailgate. "I wasn't scared," he said defensively. "I thought I had scared you."

"You sure it wasn't my horrible nudity that made you scream?"

"Are you fishing for compliments, Jane?" He grabbed the box in one arm and the open basket of pecans in the other. Jane picked up the smaller box of beans.

"Maybe just a little one. So I know you wouldn't mind if I came back."

"Well, you don't have to worry about having to save me from the bottom of a whiskey bottle anymore."

"You didn't quite make it to the bottom. I poured the rest out."

He shook his head. "I'm an idiot. As far as coming to the apartment, you are always welcome. Any time, day or night. If I change my mind, I'll move the key." He walked toward the restaurant, and Jane held the door open.

"You won't. You're too nice," she said as he walked through.

He didn't respond, and doubt pecked at her. They had lost their easy rapport, and it was her fault.

"Where did you get those pecans? It's too early in the season." Amber stood next to the counter with a batch of bread dough in her floured hands.

"I brought them from storage. Do you want them?"

"Heck, yeah, I want them. I've had so many orders for pecan rolls, I'm going to run out before October. Do you have any more?"

"Twenty gallons of shelled in the freezer." Bo set the produce in the front corner where they had several shelves set up for locally grown fruits and vegetables.

"I'll take them all."

"You can have half of them. I give you all of my pecans, you'll start baking pecan specialty desserts, and I won't get any pecan waffles until November when the new harvest comes in."

"Want a pecan waffle now? Jane can fix you up, can't you, Jane?"

"Sure," Jane said.

"I better not. I'd love some coffee to go, though."

"Coming right up." Jane picked up a disposable coffee cup and filled it with the coffee from the carafe. She handed it to him, and his fingers brushed hers in the exchange.

"Thank you."

Thumpity. Thumpity. Thumpity went her heart when he nodded to her and turned on his heel to leave. Jane watched him go, feeling the rush of blood through her body with the rapid heartbeat. Her skin warmed, and she took a couple of deep breaths. He opened the truck door, but on the passenger side. What was he doing? Reaching inside, he backed out holding something in his hand then entered the restaurant again. He marched over to her and held out his hand, giving her a small flashlight.

"I've been meaning to give this to you. When you go out at night, take this with you. It's a key ring that has a flashlight and a small canister of mace. That way you can see where you're going and maybe defend yourself if somebody tries to grab you." He raised his hand to Amber in farewell and strode back out the door.

Going to his truck, he entered and slid in the driver side. Lowering the visor, he caught the keys he must have stored there. Then the engine started up, and in a moment, he was gone.

Jane turned, and saw Amber watching her.

"Huh," she said.

"What?" Jane asked.

Amber lifted her chin a bit toward the door. "Him."

"Bo?"

"Yeah. What's going on with him and you?"

Jane shrugged. What was going on with her and Bo? She liked him. Really liked him, yes. Her heart racing when he looked at her and the tenderness she felt when she watched him the other night quote Shakespeare made her wonder if it was more than like. Maybe she was falling in love with him. Would that be so bad?

She shivered. "He's nice."

"Nice." Amber smiled. "You've met his mother."

"Yes."

"You like her?"

"I suppose so. I don't know her very well."

"MayLynn? In the pros and cons of Bo Anderson, she's the only con you got to worry about."

Chapter Twelve

Bo stood on the porch of the little house and knocked on the door. The door swung inward after a minute, and Laura stood there. Her hair was mussed as if she had been lying down. "Hi. Jane isn't here."

"I know." Uneasiness ran through Bo. "I just left the diner."

"Oh. Is that where she is?" She wiped her eye with one hand.

"Yes. She's helping with breakfast. I hope I didn't wake you."

"I don't sleep too well. Haven't for a long time."

"Is it okay if I come inside?"

"I don't have any coffee. Jane usually makes it when she's here."

"I've already had some, thanks."

Laura stepped back, and Bo walked inside.

She gestured to the couch. "Have a seat."

Bo nodded and sat on one side. Laura sat on the other side.

"So, what's this about? You want to work out the details of us staying?"

"No. Not really. I was wondering…about my dad."

Laura studied him for a few seconds. "Zachary and I were good friends. He was about five years older than me growing up, and I followed him around like a puppy."

"For how long?"

"Oh, I guess until I was about twelve or so and realized he was a boy and I was a girl, and we were too old to go skinny dipping together. He still came around, but it wasn't too long after that he met your mother, and well, that was it."

"What do you mean?"

"Oh, he fell head over heels in love with her. Not that anybody could blame him. She was beautiful. The most beautiful woman I'd ever seen. When I saw her, I came back here and cried my eyes out. I knew there was no hope that he'd ever look at me like I saw him looking at her. With his heart in his eyes."

"So, you were in love with him."

"As much as a twelve year old could be, I suppose. But I got over it. By the time they married, it didn't mean anything to me other than I hoped Zachary was happy. Your mama is high maintenance, but I imagine you know that about her."

Bo studied Laura closely. He wanted the truth. The whole ugly truth. "But you and he were still friends."

"Well, sure. He'd come over every once in a while, and we'd go fishing or something like that. One time MayLynn found us out at the fishing hole. Oh, my gosh, she was madder than a hornet. She started picking up rocks and throwing them at us. Your daddy was so cute. 'Now, MayLynn,' he said. 'Darlin', you know there ain't nobody but you. Laura and I is just trying to catch some catfish for supper.' She pelted him right here." Laura held her finger to her forehead. "And he kept coming toward her like she was the queen bee, and he was one of her little worker bees. Blood running down his forehead. He didn't care."

Bo squeezed his eyes shut. He'd seen that scar on Zachary's forehead, just above his eyebrow. He'd never asked him how it happened. It hadn't occurred to him to wonder.

"He was crazy about MayLynn. He and I were just friends." Laura pinned him with her stare. "Nothing more."

"You'd tell me, wouldn't you, if it wasn't so?"

"Well, now, she'd probably tell you different. She was convinced he and I were sleeping together, but we never did. He was faithful to her, as far as I knew. And even after I went off to college, I doubt he ever loved anyone else. Nobody existed for him except MayLynn." Her mouth tilted up on one side.

"What about her?"

"What?"

"Was my mom faithful to him?"

Laura's eyes narrowed at him. "Who have you been talking to, boy?"

"My mother."

"I can't say what your mother did or didn't do," Laura said briskly. "As you can imagine, we weren't close."

"Even though you were second cousins?"

Laura pressed her lips together and did a raspberry. "My granddaddy was a bootlegger. He ran shine all over this part of Alabama. He was ostracized by the Voyles family. My granny was a good Christian woman, certainly, but the rest of the Voyles were teetotalers, and you know there were two Baptist preachers in the family. Only thing worse than drinking was dancing." She lowered her chin and peered at Bo. "And getting caught doing either one of them was the worse sin of all. Granny got thrown out of the Baptist church, but by God, the little Anglican church on Forest Avenue welcomed her in, and she served on the Guild for the rest of her life. Mama continued the tradition of embarrassing the family when she ran off with a jailbird, and even though he never committed another crime the rest of his life, well, they just couldn't stand to have someone like that on the family tree. We were what you might call black sheep."

"Your dad spent time in prison?"

"Yeah. Nothing serious. He got drunk one night and stole a car. He went joyriding and crashed it into Joseph Brown's cow. Killed the cow and totaled the car, so Joe pressed charges, and Daddy spent about six months in prison then had a suspended license for a year after that. But he learned his lesson. I never saw him drink a drop of alcohol my whole life, and any time any of his buddies was drinking, he'd drive them home. I'd hear the phone ring in the middle of the night, and he'd leave and come back a little while later. Mama said it was his taxi service to the community. Sort of a way he gave back to the town for the sins of his past."

"Was my mama close to your dad?"

"I…I don't know, Bo. I never saw them together."

"You know what I'm getting at, though, right?"

"We were all neighbors. Sometimes you get together with your neighbors. Like we're talking today."

"What was your dad like?"

"He was a good man."

Bo waited for her to say more, but she didn't. Frustration bubbled within him. Didn't Laura know what information he needed from her?

"Did Zachary ever tell you he was worried about my mom leaving him?"

"MayLynn would never have left Zachary. Oh, my gosh, the way he made over her. She would have been crazy to do so."

She is crazy, Bo thought. He arched an eyebrow at Laura.

"You know what I mean. Not crazy like MayLynn crazy, but crazy as in she would have never done it."

"Not even with someone close by—like a…neighbor?"

Laura shook her head. "No. MayLynn loved Zachary, almost as much as he loved her. You are so much like him, it's almost hard to look at you."

"I never thought I looked much like either of my parents."

"You have Zachary's eyes and his strong chin."

Bo rested his forearms on his knees. "What color were your dad's eyes?"

"He had brown eyes. Soulful eyes, my mom used to say."

"Maybe Isaiah and MayLynn had a friendship like you and my dad." He watched for her response.

"Oh." Laura waved her hand in dismissal. "All of that was a long time ago. I only saw Zachary a couple of times after I went off to college. We moved away shortly after then, and as you know, my dad had agreed not to come back here."

"Does that agreement strike you as odd?"

"A lot of things strike me as odd."

Bo continued to press her. "Why would Zachary make an agreement with Isaiah to sell him land for thirty-five years but not allow him to live on it?"

"Who knows why they did it."

Bo stared at her hard, looking for any clue that she was his sister and that she knew it. "I think I know."

She threw her hands up. "Well, what's the point in ruminating over it? It's done. They worked it out, and it seemed to suit them both well enough. And it probably would have still suited everybody, except I got this notion to come back here and live out my days in this old shack that I called home many years ago."

If Laura hadn't come back, Bo would never have found out the man he called Dad his whole life wasn't really his dad after all.

How could she have done this?

"Is your mama giving you a hard time about me being here?"

Bo looked down at the worn floor.

"She loved your daddy very much. You know that, right? I bet it nearly killed her when he died."

"She has never gotten over it."

Laura reached over and patted his shoulder. "You poor thing. You had to deal with losing your father and having to take the burden of your mother's grief as well. That was hard, wasn't it?"

"It wasn't so bad."

"I was an only child. I know what it's like. They say an only child is spoiled, but we're not. We have to live up to all of the expectations both our parents have for us. No one else to blame anything on. No one else to lighten the load. All of the love, dreams, legacies, family history, and baggage gets dumped on that one child."

Bo sighed. Yes. It was a lot of baggage to shoulder.

"I had wanted to have more than one child because I

didn't want to do that to my own son. We did have another son, but he died when he was a baby, and I never could have any more children."

"I'm sorry."

"Thank you. Jane is like a daughter to me. She was an orphan. Did she tell you?"

Bo didn't answer.

"I can't really imagine what she must have gone through before she came into our lives. I know they found her in Texas not too far from the Mexican border. They never found her parents or anyone who knew how she got there, so they called her Jane Doe, and she went into foster care. From the time she was maybe two years old to when she turned eighteen, she went from foster family to foster family. What a sad plight for a little girl, to never know where she came from or who she was. But she was a good wife to my son, and she's been mighty good to me."

Laura's wise eyes gazed on Bo until he had to stop himself from squirming. "That girl never knew her daddy or her mama, but it doesn't negate the incredibly giving and kind person she is. If her past had been different, I probably wouldn't have her as my family. In fact, I probably would have perished in the fire that killed my husband and son. The past is the past. What you're doing now. That's what matters."

****

It was past nine in the evening. Laura was lying on the couch. The television was on, but the sound was muted.

Jane held her tennis shoes by her fingers and thumb as she strode into the room and pulled out a chair from the table. She sat down and began putting on her shoes. Laura rose up on an elbow. "Where are you going?"

"I'm going to look for Bo. He's still not answering his phone. I stopped by his apartment earlier, but I guess he was still working."

"Didn't you see him this morning?"

"How do you know that?"

Laura smirked. "Didn't you tell me?"

"No."

"Hmm. I could have sworn you did."

"Nope." Jane waited for the other woman to say how she knew, but she didn't. "Did he come out here looking for me?"

"I don't know why he came out here. Maybe he was looking for you."

Jane finished tying her shoes. "I want to try to make up for jumping on him about the eviction. I don't think he had anything to do with it."

"Probably not." Laura frowned. "Is that what you're going to wear?"

Jane looked down at her blue jeans and shirt. "What?"

"Go put on that sundress. The white one with the embroidery."

"Why?"

"Because you look pretty in it. You do want to look pretty for him, don't you?"

"Well," Jane shifted on one foot and stretched her leg. "I suppose. I don't think he notices things like that."

"Really? He's a man, isn't he? I was on the roof the day he came over here, puffing up his chest around Miles like a rooster."

"Ugh. Don't compare him to a rooster."

"You know, I used to hear a rooster crow every once in a while. I haven't heard it for several days."

"Maybe MayLynn finally got her wish."

"What?"

"Nothing. I'm leaving. I won't be gone long."

"Go change first. Hurry up. You want to see him, don't you?"

Jane stood for a moment, torn between obeying Laura and going ahead and leaving so she could find Bo sooner.

"Go on." Laura made a shooing motion with her hand.

Jane turned around and went into her bedroom. She changed clothes and came back into the room. She held out her arms. "Happy?"

Laura sat up and placed her feet on the floor. "Get

your brush."

"Why do you want me to get all dolled up for Bo?"

"Because he likes you, and I think you deserve to have some fun."

"I don't want him to be mad at us."

"He's not. He's a good man. Just like his daddy."

Jane knew Laura meant Zachary. She retrieved her brush and sat on the edge of the couch. Handing the brush over her shoulder to Laura, she dutifully sat still while her mother-in-law brushed her hair. In a moment, Jane's body relaxed at the older woman's pampering.

"Your hair is so pretty. As black as coal and so soft."

"Coal isn't pretty."

"Sure it is. When they mine it, it's iridescent. So shiny, you'd think it was an ebony jewel."

Jane shook her head at the knowledge Laura often tapped into. Laura set the brush down. "Go find him. I'll call you if I need you, so don't hurry home and don't worry about me."

"I suppose I'll drive. He says he worries when I go out at night by myself." Jane paused at the door. "You sure you're okay?"

"Really okay." She patted the pillow and leaned back on it. "Have a good time."

In a few minutes, Jane was at the barn. Bo's truck was there again, and once again there were no lights in the window above. Jane grasped the key and pulled it from the nail then walked up the stairs. Peering in the window, she saw the apartment was completely dark. She knocked at the door and waited for any summons. But none came.

She took a fortifying breath and inserted the key in the lock, turned it, and opened the door.

Chapter Thirteen

Jane's heart pounded in her chest. It was really dark in the apartment. Other than the café window on the front door, the only other natural light came from skylights in the roof. With the cloud-ridden night sky, no light shone in even though the moon was full. Jane reached into her purse and pulled out the flashlight Bo had given her.

What do I want to accomplish here?

He was probably asleep. Waking him up to apologize seemed silly. But if he was sleeping, maybe Jane could look at his foot for the birthmark. She'd know then if he was Laura's half-brother.

What if he was? Would it change anything?

It's not any of my business.

Jane turned back toward the door. A slight rustling made her pause. She looked over her shoulder.

"Bo?" she said in a low voice.

Nothing.

She pivoted and stealthily crossed to the open doorway that was his bedroom. With her hand covering most of the glow coming from the small flashlight, she stepped in the room. A low light from the bathroom's partially open door illuminated Bo's bed, and Bo's form covered with the comforter Jane had seen the day she'd bathed here. The comforter was pulled to one side exposing a corner of the sheet-covered mattress and Bo's toes on one foot. Laura and Mandy's birthmark had been on the right foot. Jane was pretty sure the toes peeking from the cover were from his left foot. Still, if she were very quiet, she ought to be able to see the mark, if it was there.

She approached the bed, watching closely for any indication he was awake. There was an odd sweet smell in the room she couldn't quite place. Kneeling on the floor, she flinched when her knees creaked. Reaching forward, she pinched the comforter and inched it upward. Using the comforter as a barrier for the flashlight, she craned her head to see the top of his feet.

"Jane?" Bo's sleepy voice said. He sat up and the comforter slipped out of her grasp. She shut off the flashlight.

"Hi, Bo."

"What are you doing?"

"Umm. Trying to…look at your feet."

He moved, and the lamp on the bedside table came on. No shirt.

He had on no shirt.

His shirts had hidden well-developed muscles and a chest, the skin slightly paler below his neck in the sexiest farmer's tan—the only one, actually—Jane had ever seen.

The comforter in front of her moved catching her attention until the bottoms of both of his feet were exposed. Jane realized he had pulled the covers off of them.

"All right."

Jane looked from his feet to his face. "What?"

"You wanted to look at my feet. There they are." He wiggled his toes. "Want to sit on the bed? You can see them better. How come you want to look at my feet?"

"Umm." Jane stood up and sat on the edge of the bed. She held onto the footboard with one hand. The comforter covered from above his ankles to his waist. Was he wearing shorts?

Please let him have something on under that comforter.

Jane examined the tops of his feet. Skin. Hair. No birthmarks.

"I was…" She sighed in relief…or something. Placing her hand on one foot, she curled her fingers around the arch of it. "You have very nice feet."

"Thanks. Anything else you want to see?"

Jane laughed, and he smiled in response. "I'm sorry." She squeezed his foot. "This must seem really weird to you."

"Yeah." He yawned. "Sorry. I worked about twelve hours in the fields today, and I pretty much came in, jumped in the shower, and then went to bed."

She stood up. "I shouldn't have—"

"Don't go." He stretched then froze. "Ouch."

"What's wrong?"

"I spent the last two days picking tomatoes. It kills my back, but our extra workers aren't coming in until the beans are ready. That's when we really need the help."

Aha. She recognized the smell. It was muscle cream.

"I could…" Jane hesitated. "I could give you a back rub."

"As tempting as that is, I'm going to pass. You'll end up with Ben Gay all over your hands, and it doesn't come off very easily. Tell you what. Why don't you step into the living room for a few minutes, and I'll get up, throw on some clothes, and join you."

"You're naked."

"Well, yeah, since you mention it."

Jane jumped up as if she'd been burnt. "I shouldn't have come. I'm sorry." She hurried out of the room.

She heard the movement of the bedclothes and his footsteps. "It's all right. Really. Have a seat in there, and you can tell me what's on your mind."

Jane stood at the door and looked out the window. Lightning lit up the sky behind a heavy cloud near the horizon, and a light drizzle of rain pattered on the balcony. She heard Bo come up behind her.

"It's raining a little bit."

The light in the small foyer came on, and when she turned around Bo was walking into the sitting area. He wore blue jeans and a T-shirt. He sat on the big leather couch and propped his bare feet on the ottoman. She walked into the room.

"Did you hear me? About the rain?"

"Yes. Rain is good. I suppose your prayer worked."

"God worked. God made it rain."

Bo didn't reply. Jane settled in the corner of the couch. "Would you forgive me for accusing you of evicting Laura and me?"

He bent his knees and dropped his feet to the floor. "There's nothing to forgive. I'm sorry it happened. Really sorry, Jane. My mother…" He sighed. "She's got some things going on which I…didn't know about until recently, and I'm afraid Laura and you are suffering because of the residue from it." He rubbed the bridge of his nose with his thumb and his forefinger.

The fatigue in the gesture tore at Jane. Perhaps she and Laura were seeing the residue from it, but Jane had no doubt Bo was catching the brunt of it.

"I'm sure MayLynn did what she thought was best for her and you, your family. Laura is thinking coming here was probably a mistake. Her dad had told her she could never go back, but she thought he just meant it would never feel like home again."

Bo shook his head. He stared at a spot on the carpet, and a sad expression settled so heavily on his face that it scared Jane.

She scooted over the cushion close to him and took his hand. "Bo?"

He looked at her, the desolation evident in his eyes.

"Tell me. Please tell me what's going on," Jane urged.

He closed his eyes and bowed his head. Jane gripped his hand tighter, and his fingers clung to hers. She couldn't hint at what could have been true—that she knew MayLynn had had an affair with Isaiah and that Isaiah could be his father. Not until he told her what he suspected. Because if she was wrong about him knowing, then she could make whatever burdened him even worse.

She moved her head close to his. "Whatever it is, I'll listen. I won't judge. I understand about terrible things, about not knowing and living through it. I do, Bo."

"Jane. Jane." He whispered. "I don't know anything anymore. I thought I knew my parents, my family, my life, but I didn't. I don't. They kept things from me, and if y'all hadn't come here, I would have lived my entire life not knowing."

"Everyone has secrets. Things we wish weren't true, but are. You're the same person you were before. So what if the land has belonged to someone else all these years? You get it back in a few years, right? In fact, Laura broke the contract. You can have it now if you want it. She'd like to live in the house, but you weren't using the house anyway."

Bo turned his head and looked at Jane. "I think Laura is my half-sister."

"Why do you think that?"

"Because MayLynn slept with Laura's father and then got pregnant with me." He said it so calmly, so evenly, as if he were talking about someone else's life. It worried Jane.

"You're not Isaiah's son," Jane whispered. "At least, Laura doesn't think so."

"How could she know? I asked her, and she said she didn't know what happened between her dad and MayLynn."

"There's a mark. A birthmark on Laura's foot. My husband Mandy had it too. It's a red mark—very distinctive on the top of the foot. Laura says it's a Justice trait. If you were Isaiah's son, you'd have the mark, but you don't. That's what I was looking for."

Bo straightened. His mouth fell open in shock.

Jane reached down to his jean-clad leg, and he allowed her to pull up his foot and rest it on the ottoman. "If you had it, it would be right here. But see? All you have is skin and a patch of hair. No birthmark. You're not a Justice."

He lifted his other foot and examined both feet carefully. No birthmarks on either foot. He slid them back to the floor. "You really wanted to look at my feet."

"I know it was none of my business, and it was a terrible imposition into your personal life, but it would be kind of neat to have another close family member. I never had a family before Mandy, and when he and his father died, I not only lost them, but it took away my dream to have the family I've always wanted. Laura thought she was dying before she came here, and it scared me because she's all I have now. At least if you'd had the birthmark, you and MayLynn could be part of our family too, or we could be part of yours. I know it's selfish to have wanted that, but I…I guess I'll have to be content to have you as cousins."

Bo sat back on the couch, and with his hand, he pulled Jane with him and tucked her into his side. For a long time, they sat there together like that. Jane could feel his heart beating near her head. Her body moved with the motion of his breathing, and she began to breathe with him.

Inhale. Exhale. Inhale. Exhale.

He relaxed, and she relaxed into him surrounded by the aroma of Ben Gay and Bo, the softness of his cotton shirt, the hardness of the muscles beneath, and the firm band of his arm around her shoulders.

Inhale. Exhale. Inhale. Exhale.

His arm loosened, and he looked down at her. "Would you mind if I kissed you, Cousin Jane?"

She shook her head. "No."

He had begun to move his face closer to hers but stopped. "No, you wouldn't mind, or no, don't do it."

"No, I wouldn't mind. Yes, please do it."

He smiled and placed that smile on her mouth, and Jane inhaled, feeling the softness of his lips and the rasp of a day's growth of beard against her skin.

Oh my gosh. I'm really doing this.

Jane clutched at Bo's shirt, not sure whether she wanted to pull him closer or push him away.

Bo broke the kiss and tilted his head back a fraction. "I thought you came into the bedroom because you wanted to make love."

Jane laughed. "And, of course, you didn't want to."

"Who says I didn't? Why do you think I made you leave before I got out of the bed? I didn't want to embarrass myself."

"If you weren't opposed to it, why did you turn down the back rub?"

"I told you. I had Ben Gay on my back. If you're going to be pawing my other parts, I didn't want it all over your hands."

"Pawing your other parts, huh? Oh my, Bo. You do have a way with words." She ran her fingers along his jaw and nuzzled him. "Is it all right if we kiss again?"

He nodded, and Jane touched her lips to his, tasting and exploring. She felt his hands pick her up and settle her on his lap without losing contact with her mouth. It felt good. He felt good.

After a while, he stopped again. "Jane?" he whispered close to her ear.

She quivered at the sound of her name, so soft, on his lips. "Yes, Bo."

"I want to do this all night, but my head's spinning. It's a lot to take in. Know what I mean?"

Emotion filled Jane's chest. "Yes."

He nuzzled her cheek. "If you stay here, I won't want to stop, and we need to. I need to."

"I understand."

"Let me take you home, and we can talk some more tomorrow. Kiss some more tomorrow, I hope. A lot more."

"All right."

With hands held, he guided her down the staircase. The rain had stopped. Jane drove to the house, and Bo rode in the passenger seat, saying he'd walk back to the barn. He walked her to the stairs and placed his hand on the tree.

"Hey," he said.

"Yes?"

"What do you think of carving our initials on this tree? That way when Miles come back, he'll know that you and I are an item."

"Are we an item?" Jane asked.

Bo shrugged. "Are we? Forty-five minutes worth of kissing ought to count for something."

"It's just wood. I guess if you change your mind, I

could cut the tree down." He'd changed his mind about Amber, after all. Perhaps he'd change his mind about her as well.

"Laura's not going to let you cut that tree down," he declared, quite happily, she thought.

Jane shrugged. "Well, we'll just cut that chunk out of it then."

"What if I don't change my mind? What if you change yours?"

"We'll still be cousins."

"Cousins with their initials in a heart." He put his hand in his pants and took out a pocketknife. "I'm really going to do it, so if you think it's a dumb idea, you better say something." He opened the blade.

"I don't think it's a dumb idea. Do it."

He looked at the tree. "How about here. Right in the front."

"No. On the side here. It's not really our tree. It's Laura's. I don't know how she'd feel about having a heart on the front announcing to every visitor that her daughter-in-law has a boyfriend."

"On the back."

"Okay, then I can see it every time I go out of the house."

Bo whittled the bark off the spot Jane had indicated. "I could still be her brother."

"She says you look a lot like Zachary," Jane replied.

Bo cut a fat heart in the pale soft wood underneath.

Jane watched his work, warmth budding in her chest. "That's a beautiful heart. How many of these have you carved?"

"This is my first." He carved a J and an S.

"Thanks. I get to be on top. I like that."

He arched an eyebrow at her. "You're talking about your initials, right?"

She chuckled. "That's what I'm looking at."

He added a plus sign then his own initials underneath. "There. Now we're official."

****

Jane had planned on driving over to the apartment the next morning before dawn, but it was the sound of Bo's truck that woke her up. By the time she made it to the front of the house, a light knock sounded on the door. She opened it and saw the back of Bo. He pivoted and looked back at her. Stepping out of the way, he pointed to the tree with a grin.

"It's still there. We're still official."

Happiness erupted in her chest. "It's only been a few hours. What did you think was going to happen?"

"That maybe it was a dream."

She shook her head.

"Or that I cornered you into kissing me when all you really wanted was to look at my feet."

She shook her head again.

"Or that you had changed your mind."

The hopeful light in Bo's gaze overcame Jane. She lowered her eyes to his shirtfront because she was afraid he'd see her love for him. At least, she thought she loved him. Last night after she'd come in the house, she'd lain awake and relived the warmth of being in his arms on his couch, of his tenderness, the care he'd shown for her and Laura, every single thing he'd done to help them, to welcome them. Jane had examined the feelings to be sure they weren't gratitude or loyalty in response to what he'd done.

And maybe that was part of it. But it was more than that. It was the feeling of seeking him out, of wanting to start the morning with him, or yearning to be with him when she couldn't sleep at night. Wondering what he was doing in the middle of the day and wishing she could work side by side with him in the field. If she told him that, he was liable to laugh in her face. The depth of feeling scared her a little bit, because if he decided he didn't love her back or if he fell out of love like he had with Amber, then he'd break her heart.

"I haven't changed my mind," she said softly.

He wrapped his arms around her and bent his head down close to her.

"I'm glad," he said just before he touched her lips. Jane opened her mouth to his and tasted coffee on his tongue. She felt his fingers tugging on her ponytail, and then her hair was free from the band. She gripped the front of his shirt when her knees began to wobble. All too soon, he withdrew.

"I've got to go."

"All right."

"Can I take you and Laura out tonight?"

"She hasn't felt like getting out lately. She seems to get tired in the evenings. You could come over here if you like. I could fix us something."

"Sounds great. What time?"

"What time is good for you?"

"Is eight too late? I'm trying to use all the sunlight I can."

"Eight is fine."

Bo leaned forward and kissed the tip of her nose. "Eight o'clock. It's a date."

"I'm not sure it counts as a date if my mother-in-law is at the table."

Bo bypassed the tree and walked down the stairs. "Sure it does. Refer to the heart on the tree. That makes it a date."

****

Jane knocked on the front door of the Anderson house, but no one answered. She shifted the basket to her other hand and decided to walk around the back to see if MayLynn was in her flower garden. She crossed through the hedge and the arbor, feeling a little like the girl, Mary, in the book *The Secret Garden*. MayLynn wasn't on the patio, and the back door was shut with the blinds down. The beauty of the flowers drew Jane, and she set the basket on the table and strolled over to the plants. She entered the first row and strolled through, pausing occasionally to touch a petal or sniff a blossom. She was crouched next to some flowers that looked a lot like feathers.

"What are you doing here?" MayLynn's cold voice asked.

Jane looked up. The woman stood at the end of the row, her arms crossed over her chest.

Jane straightened. "I brought your basket back."

"I see it. You brought it back. Why are you still here?"

"I'm sorry. I shouldn't have hung around without you outside. It's just…your flowers are so pretty. What are these things here?"

MayLynn marched toward her. "Those are…cockscombs."

Jane giggled. "Are you kidding? You'd have a flower in the garden called cockscomb? As much as you hate roosters?"

MayLynn's lip quivered, as if she were suppressing a smile. "The actual name is Celosia. I figured you wouldn't know that name."

"They don't even look real. My gosh, it's hard to believe they come in all of these colors."

"Yes." She walked down the row and stepped onto another path. "Come here and look at these."

Jane followed her and saw bright frilly flowers.

"This is also Celosia. See why they would call it cockscomb?"

"Yes. Other than the bright colors, it doesn't look at all like the other flower."

"That's because you don't know what you're looking at." She tapped her foot a couple of times. "So, have you…seen Bo lately?"

The question raised a warning flag. "Yes," Jane answered carefully. "I saw him last night."

"I suppose he's staying out at his barn."

"Yes. At least, last night he was there."

The older woman's mouth thinned. "You and Laura being here is creating a lot of problems. Do you know that?"

"I'm…sorry."

"Why did she have to come back? Did she think that Zachary was still here? Was she going to try to—"

"No. She thought she was dying. She wanted to come home to die."

MayLynn's eyes widened. "What?"

"This man came by selling burial plots, and she got this idea she really was going to die, and we really haven't had a home since the fire. I think she feels safe here."

MayLynn snorted. "That's ironic. Her safety is costing me my family."

"Why?"

The older woman glared at her. "I don't have to talk to you about this. You know nothing about how awful all of this has been."

"No, ma'am. You certainly don't have to talk to me about any of this, and you're probably right. I don't know how us being here has been stressful to you. Laura just wanted a quiet familiar place to be, and this is the only place she has anymore."

"It's not hers." MayLynn bit the words out, as if she were speaking with her jaw wired shut. "It was just an agreement between two idiot men a long time ago."

Jane cocked her head to the side inquisitively. "What do you wish they had done? Do you wish your husband had handled it differently?"

MayLynn brought her hand to her face and covered her mouth, as if to suppress a sob. Jane had seen that look of dejection on Bo's face the night before.

Jane continued. "Was there a better way it could have worked out back then?"

"No," MayLynn whispered. "No."

"But it was still very painful. Whatever it was."

MayLynn stared in front of her. Lost in some distant memory. She began to walk toward the patio. "Tell Bo. Tell him I'm sorry."

"MayLynn?"

The older woman stopped, but she didn't turn around.

"I don't mind telling Bo you're sorry, but don't you

think it would be better coming from you?"

"Bo's not speaking to me anymore." MayLynn walked on onto the patio and into the house, shutting the door behind her.

Chapter Fourteen

Jane thought about what MayLynn had said as she drove back to the house. Laura was sitting on a lawn chair on the porch.

"Hi," Jane said as she hugged the tree to climb the stairs.

"Hi, yourself."

"Is Miles gone?"

"Yeah. He said he was going to get some lunch, and he'd be back this afternoon."

Jane leaned against the railing, testing it with her hands before she put too much weight on it. "Maybe he'll finish the floor today."

"Maybe." The older woman crossed her legs and watched Jane. "I noticed some new graffiti on my tree."

"Oh?" Jane felt a smile break out on her face.

"Guess you know what I'm talking about."

"I hope you don't mind. Bo wanted to put it right in front. I suggested the side where it wouldn't be so visible, so we compromised and put it on the back."

"He's establishing his territory, I guess."

"It's partially your fault, making me dress up and fix my hair for him."

"You love him?"

"I'm a little scared to think too much about it."

"Jump in, Jane. Life is so precious. We both know that."

"Yes. Yes, we do."

Laura stood up. She reached forward and kissed Jane on the cheek. "This makes me very happy. Happy for you."

"It's just a heart carved on a tree."

"The tree will grow."

"I hope so, Laura."

"You both are good people. It will grow. You'll see."

****

Jane looked through the windshield of the cab of the tractor. She shifted on Bo's lap, and one of his hands rested on her hip while the other one was wrapped around her waist.

"Don't you think you ought to be steering?" she asked.

"No. You're steering."

"But I don't know what I'm doing."

"You're doing fine. Just ask Jonathan." Bo pressed a button on the radio to call him.

Bo had told her Jonathan was working in the field up the hill from where they were and had a great view of their progress. "Hey, Jon. How's Miss Jane doing?"

"Just fine," was the reply.

"How are her lines?"

"Mostly straight."

Bo grinned at Jane. "See? I told you."

"He said mostly straight. That means they're not straight."

"Don't look at me. Watch the horizon. Otherwise, you're going to go from mostly straight to curlicues."

"I'm not good at this."

"You're good enough, and this is your first time. I think you're doing great for the first time. And besides, it's just hay. It doesn't have to be perfect. If you leave a few tufts here and there, it's okay."

Jane looked behind her and looked at the big rectangular thing cutting the grass and compressing it in small rectangular shapes. She couldn't remember what anything was called and didn't want to ask Bo again.

"How come you don't grow crops on this part of the land?"

"Because Mama likes grass close to the house so Daddy always gave her a few acres of grass, and we could make hay bales and sell it to townies for different things. It's not as efficient to bale it this way if you're feeding cows, but city folks think this is what hay should look like and it's easier for them to haul it, so we bale it and sell it to them. All right. We're coming to the end of the row. You remember what to do?"

"I let you steer."

"Well, you could do that, but we're going to shift gears, so look behind you and watch what the baler's doing."

Jane put her hand on Bo's shoulder and attempted to look behind her. He reached up and kissed her on the lips.

"It's tight in here. I can't see anything."

"I like it."

"Yeah, well, you could probably do this blindfolded. I wish you didn't trust me so much."

His hand tightened on her middle. "The bale is done, so turn it off there."

Jane followed his instructions.

"That's good. Let's check in with Jonathan and let him know what we're doing." Bo talked to him through the radio mounted in the cab.

"How come you don't just use your cell phone?"

"Service is spotty. The radios are more reliable."

"We're going in," he said to the other man. "Finish up, and let's meet over on the west patch. Okay?"

"Ten-four."

"What's that mean?" Jane asked.

"It means he heard what I said," Bo responded patiently.

"Oh."

His arm tightened around her. "Having fun?"

"Yes. This is fun."

He smiled, and Jane's heart flippity-flopped. "Good."

"Why don't we stop in and visit MayLynn?"

The smile fell. "Not right now."

"How come?"

"Because I need to get you home, and I need to get over to check on our Silver Queen corn. We planted it early because I was hoping it could be done by the middle of the month."

"I might stop in and see her. I can walk home from there."

He shook his head. "It's two miles."

"Two miles won't take me half an hour to walk, and that's going slow," she countered.

"It's too hot to walk."

"No, it's not."

Bo shook his head and rolled his eyes. Jane smiled. The eye roll meant she just got her way.

"Ten minutes," he declared. "I can't stay longer than that."

She moved his hand to the steering wheel then turned to him. She kissed his neck. "Thank you, Bo."

"Hopefully, you'll thank me properly later," he grumbled.

****

The hinges squeaked as the door opened, and Bo resisted the urge to get out the WD-40 and oil it.

But if he didn't do it, who would?

Not your problem right now, a voice said.

She's lied to me my whole life. She's just going to have to live with squeaky hinges for a while.

Bo hadn't been in the house since that horrible day when MayLynn had told him she'd been catting around on his dad with the hired hand.

If Zachary Anderson was even his dad.

Uneasiness skittered up and down Bo's spine. He didn't want to be here.

"Take off your shoes," Bo counseled as he bent over and grabbed one boot to pull it from his foot. Sweet, obedient Jane didn't even question him. She immediately began taking off her tennis shoes.

"Hello."

MayLynn appeared at the kitchen door. She was dressed in her bridge clothes. Of course, it was Wednesday—the day she and her bridge friends got together in increments of four and used the excuse to fix and eat fancy hors d'oeuvres and show off their houses to each other. Bo grinned. His daddy used to pronounce it *whore de vores* just to irritate his mama.

"Oh, Bo. Please. Y'all don't have to take off your shoes."

"Since when?" Bo asked. Geez, she'd drilled that rule into his head since he was old enough to wear shoes and track in mud from outside.

Jane hesitated. Bo took off his other boot, and she followed his lead. As he had done for decades, he placed his shoes neatly inside the door. This time, he took Jane's shoes and set them next to his. They looked nice arranged beside each other.

"I'm so glad, so glad to see you." Mama's voice was hesitant, surprised, hopeful. This big house probably felt pretty empty with no one but her and the skeletons rattling around in the closets. Bo turned to his mother and saw her hesitant smile. "How nice that you all...." MayLynn looked from one to the other.

Bo could see she was putting one and one together and getting one couple. Maybe she'd noticed, too, how carefully he had arranged their pairs of shoes together.

That's right, Mama. Your son is dating a Mexican, even if she can't speak a word of Spanish.

Mama had always said she didn't like the crops near the house because she didn't want the farm hands getting too close to her flowers. Even though now, Bo realized, she obviously hadn't minded Isaiah Justice getting too close and putting his farm hands on her.

How? How could she have done that to Dad? And why the hell would he stay with her and, in essence, give away a quarter of their land that had been in the family for generations?

"Can I fix y'all some tea?"

"Sure. That'd be great," Jane said. "Bo was cutting hay and thought it would be nice to stop in since we were just up the way." She looked at him for confirmation. "Right, Bo?"

It crossed his mind to be a big, fat jerk and say it was

Jane's idea to stop in and not his, but what would it accomplish?

"That's right, darlin'," he said.

If MayLynn noticed the endearment, she didn't let on.

He reached over and grabbed Jane's hand. "Where do you want us, Mama?" he asked.

"Come sit down at the table. Do y'all want something to eat?"

Jane followed her to the table and pulled Bo with her.

"No. A glass of tea is all we can stay for," he said firmly.

"Oh." MayLynn went to the cabinet and took out three glasses. Filling them with ice from the dispenser on the fridge, she poured tea from a pitcher on the counter. Bo sat at one of the chairs and attempted to pull Jane into his lap, but she resisted and shot him a dirty look before sliding into the chair next to him.

"How have you been, son?" MayLynn asked as she set the tea in front of him and Jane.

"Just fine."

"So, are you two…dating?"

"Yes, ma'am," he answered, daring the older woman to give any clue she didn't approve. He'd walk right out of this house if she even looked at Jane wrong.

MayLynn's mouth turned up in a contented smile. "That's very nice. I heard Amber is dating that Cron boy. Seems like he's just about moved in with her. His milk truck is always at the diner these days. I guess you all parted on good terms."

"Yes. I'm still a partner in the restaurant with the produce corner."

"Why don't you and Jane come have supper with me sometime?"

Bo opened his mouth to decline.

"I really can't be away from Laura for that long, MayLynn." Jane smiled apologetically at the older woman. "I worry about her, especially in the evenings."

She blinked a few times, perhaps measuring her next

words. "Is she…all right?"

"I think so, but it's kind of lonely out there."

MayLynn turned and watched Bo, and guilt nipped at him like an annoying pup.

"Perhaps she'd want to come have supper as well."

Bo's eyes widened in shock. Had his mother just invited Laura into her house to eat at her table? Now this was an interesting development, as in completely unexpected, and anybody could have knocked Bo over with a feather because of it.

"That's very kind of you, MayLynn. That would be very nice, wouldn't it, Bo?"

"Sure, Mama. We'd love to do that."

"Wonderful. When can you come?"

****

Their breaths mingled as Bo's hand slid under Jane's skirt and across her thigh. He cupped her leg, fitting her a little more securely to him on his couch.

Jane closed her eyes, reveling in the burn of wanting all of him, the anticipation of making love, and the delicious torture of holding off. She ran her fingers inside his untucked shirt. "I better go," she whispered.

"I don't want you to go," he murmured.

"I don't want to go, but I need to. Laura's by herself, and I told her I'd be back by ten."

Bo's thumb ran over her bra. Through the thin material, her breast responded to his touch, and she grasped his hand and brought it to her mouth. She kissed his fingers. "You're making it harder for me to leave."

"Good. I don't want you to leave." He ground his pelvis into hers and kissed her once more. Jane smiled and kissed him back. She succumbed to the haze of the sensations of her body, and his. When his fingers moved under her panties and she heard her own panting, she slid off the couch and onto the floor.

"Hey," Bo said, gazing down at her. "Where are you going?"

"I'm trying to stop us before we go too far."

"What are you afraid of?" He dropped onto the floor to his knees and pulled her onto his lap.

"You breaking my heart."

"Who says you won't break mine?" He began to nibble on her neck, and his hand was under her bra cupping her breast.

"Please, Bo. I need to get back."

"Then I'll come with you," he said against her skin. Jane shivered with need.

"All right," she agreed.

He lifted his face and gazed into her eyes. He brushed his fingers across her cheek. "Really?"

"Yes, but there's something I need to tell you first."

"Okay."

"I'm not on birth control."

"That's no problem. I've got protection." He reached forward to kiss her.

Jane moved her head out of his reach. "No. No protection."

Bo stilled. "What?"

"I don't want you to use any protection. I want to get pregnant."

Bo laughed. "What?"

"I want a baby. I've wanted a baby for a long time, so if we make love, I don't want you to use a condom."

The smile that had been on his lips fell. He shook his head. "Jane, I don't think we're ready—"

"I am. I'm ready."

Bo sat back. "You're ready to have a baby. With me."

"Lots of women have babies with their boyfriends these days. It's becoming the norm."

"Well, it's not going to be the norm for me," he said defensively. "I don't plan on having any babies with anybody but my wife. I'd like to get married for a while before I start having kids."

"I don't want to wait."

"We just started dating. We've only known each other for a few months."

"You know me well enough to make love to me," she stated evenly.

"That's different."

"I don't think it is. When you make love to someone, you give them a little piece of yourself that you never get back. You'll always be connected. No matter what."

Bo shook his head. "No, you're not. That's...crazy."

Irritation prickled at Jane, but she kept calm. "Well, maybe you don't feel connected to every girl you've been with, but who I am, where I am right now, I know I will be. I want to have a baby."

"Having a baby isn't a...one person deal. A baby needs a mama and a daddy. You ought to want to have a baby with the man you're going to want to be with for the rest of your life."

"I did. But he died in a fire."

"So, what? I'm a...substitute for Mandy?"

Jane hesitated.

"Oh, no. No. No. No." Bo nudged her off his lap and stood up.

Jane folded her legs underneath her and stood up as well. "No. It's not like that."

Bo walked to the door and looked out the window. "You took a little too long to answer."

"I'd like to have a baby with you, Bo."

"And if I say no, are you going to ask Miles next?" Bo's voice echoed off the apartment walls, his anger evident. "I'm sure he'd be glad to have sex with you without any protection. As a matter of fact, he's already got a two-year-old by a woman in Gadsden."

"You're upset."

"Of course, I'm upset. I thought I was going to get to sleep with you, and instead I find out you just want a...sperm donor." He took a few deep breaths, his shoulders shrugging with the movement. "Come on," he said more calmly. "I'll take you home."

Jane followed him out the door and down the stairs. He held the passenger door open for her, and she climbed into the cab of the truck and sat on the seat. He shut the door and in a moment, he was beside her cranking the engine. In less than five minutes, he was in front of Laura's house. The headlights of his truck shone on the tree. Even though Jane couldn't see the heart with their initials, the image of it was burned into her brain.

Jane released the seat belt and shifted her body toward him. "Bo, maybe you can't understand this, but Mandy and I were saving up to buy a house. We never took a honeymoon because we wanted to put every cent we could into getting our own place. That's where we were going to have our babies and raise them and grow old together. We were saving for our future." She watched Bo's profile lit by the dashboard lights. "When Mandy died in the fire, when I lost everything but Laura, the car we were in, the suitcases we had with us, and, of course, all the money Mandy and I had saved up in the bank, well, it made me realize how precarious life can be. I don't ever want to plan ahead like that again. I don't want to put off having a family or anything else I want because I know sometimes those things don't get to happen. I want to make love to you and get you to teach me how to grow soybeans and feel our baby growing inside of me, to nurse her, and be a PTA mom, and all of those wonderful things which make me know I'm alive."

Please understand, Bo. Your heart is so big. You've got to see what I'm saying.

"Those are your terms." His statement echoed in the truck with the diesel engine reverberating in the background.

Jane smiled. In spite of this impasse they seemed to be at, it felt good to know exactly what she wanted and whom she wanted it with.

"Jane." Bo's sigh filled the truck. "I'm not there yet."

"That's okay. I just needed you to know I am."

"No protection."

"Nope." Jane reached over and kissed him on the cheek. She left the truck and went up the porch stairs without looking back.

Those are my terms.

Dinner tomorrow night at MayLynn's ought to be interesting.

Chapter Fifteen

"Let me come pick you and Laura up."

Jane held the phone to her ear while she stood at the bathroom mirror.

"We'll just meet you there. That way if you want to stay, you can."

"I don't want to stay."

The determination in Bo's voice made Jane realize he hadn't forgiven his mother for something that happened before he'd been born.

"Let me come over to the apartment, and we'll talk about it," she countered.

He wasn't having it. "What's to talk about? I'll drive over there and pick you up."

She ignored his declaration. "I'll be right over." Jane hung up. She walked into the living room. Laura was lying on the couch watching television. "Is that what you're wearing to MayLynn's house tonight?"

"I don't think I'm going. I'm tired."

Jane put her hands on her hips. "I don't ask a lot, but I am asking you to do this. You and MayLynn need to make up with each other, so we can all move on. So yes, you are going to go tonight. You're going to be nice, and you're going to be gracious, and at the end of the night, you're going to thank her, and then I'll bring you back home. Are we clear?"

Laura blinked at her. She wasn't used to Jane being so bossy. But she had enough with getting Bo over to his mother's and helping them smooth things over. She didn't need any grief from Laura.

"I'm going over to Bo's for a little bit. When I get back, be ready."

"I don't know why I have to—"

"Because she invited us. She's making an effort, and we are going to reward that good behavior. Understand?"

"I guess it doesn't matter that I feel bad," Laura groused.

"You can go and sit at somebody's table, eat, and be civil for a little while, and then you can come home and sleep." Jane picked up her purse. "Call me if you need me."

She drove over to Bo's apartment, ready to argue with the other most important person in her life. She skipped up the stairs and knocked on the door.

Bo came to the door. "Why'd you knock?"

He was wearing a crisp, button-down shirt and his hair was wet. He must have just taken a shower. She smelled a sweet, tangy smell she was pretty sure was his cologne.

"You smell really good," she said.

"Is that supposed to distract me from the impending argument?" He walked back into the apartment.

"Our first argument."

"I think our first argument was when you told me you wanted me to be your baby daddy."

Jane followed him in the apartment, closing the door behind her. "That wasn't really an argument. Just me laying my cards on the table."

"How many kids do you want? Just one?" He stopped at the sink and turned on the faucet. Picking up a glass, he caught some water in it.

At least three, but she wasn't sure how Bo would take that.

He raised the glass to his lips, turning to her as he did so. He shook his head in amazement. "That many, huh?"

"Well, I don't want to seem greedy. Right now, I probably couldn't afford more than one."

"Except for if you had one with me, you wouldn't have to worry about whether you could afford it or not." He drank the water and set the glass on the counter.

"You've been thinking about this a lot."

"How could I not? You've got your plan worked out,

and the father of your offspring is apparently just an afterthought."

Jane didn't take the bait he dangled. She leaned back against the counter. "Until I met you, I had given up on thinking I would ever get to have any babies."

"It didn't cross your mind with Miles?"

Jane chuckled. "Why are you so jealous of Miles?"

"Because he asked you out right in front of me."

"I'm pretty sure you were still dating Amber at the time."

"Did you consider him as a potential sperm donor?" Bo asked, irritation in his tone.

"No." She laughed at the absurdity of his comment. "I wouldn't just have sex with someone to get a baby. Bo, I never really thought I'd ever be in a relationship with anyone again. This is a big step for me. I wouldn't have kept coming to visit you if I didn't feel you were someone I'd want to have children with."

"How many?" He crossed his arms over his chest, his expression tense.

"Children?"

He nodded.

"Ideally?"

"Sure."

"Four."

His eyes grew big. "Four?"

"Ideally. But it's probably too much to hope for. I never got pregnant with Mandy."

Jane pushed off the counter and stood in front of Bo. She reached a tentative hand up and stroked his cheek. He leaned his face into her hand, and she stepped closer. He closed his eyes.

"I don't want to go over to Mom's tonight." He circled his arms around her and pulled her flush against him. "I want to make love to you. But you're talking about a lifetime."

"A lifetime isn't long for some people."

"But it could be for us. It probably would be."

Oh, how she hoped so.

"I think it could be very nice." She stood on her tiptoes and lifted her face, and he bent down and placed his mouth on hers. Quickly, the kiss deepened and soon Bo had lifted her and turned her so she was sitting on the counter. Jane unbuttoned his shirt and pushed it aside then ran her lips along his shoulder.

"You're making me crazy," he whispered.

She traced a path from his shoulder to his neck, trailing little kisses on the skin there. His hand had moved under her shirt and somehow her bra was loose. His hand was warm against her flesh, and when his fingers came into contact with her nipple, the sensation was so powerful she cried out in pleasure. The sound encouraged Bo, and he lifted her shirt and suckled her. Jane held onto him. He kissed her breast and rested his face against her bare skin.

"We better stop," he said a few minutes later, his breath bringing goose bumps to her skin.

She pulled back and fastened the buttons of his shirt she had undone earlier and straightened the cloth. Then with a little difficulty she reached behind her, hooked her bra and repositioned her shirt. "I'll go get Laura and meet you there."

"Why can't we ride together?" His sweet blue eyes looked appealingly at her.

"Because you need to clear the air with her a little bit before Laura and I get there. Don't you think so?"

"She's lied to me my whole life."

Jane placed her hands on his shoulders and ran her thumbs along his muscles feeling him through the shirt. "When you were little, it wasn't something she would have, or even should have, told you. And what did you expect when you were older? How could she possibly bring it up?" She affected MayLynn's honeyed southern drawl. "Bo, honey, Mama had an affair with the farmhand, and it's possible he's your daddy." Her voice resumed its normal tone. "Is that what you wanted her to say?"

"I don't know."

"Obviously, she and Zachary worked it out a long time ago, right?"

"I guess so," he said reluctantly.

"How were they together? Did they love each other? Did they seem happy together?"

A pained expression settled on his face. "I thought so, but how can I know now?"

"Because you lived with them your whole life until your dad died. He must have forgiven her, and he was the one who needed to. Not you. You weren't even around then."

He groaned. "My life didn't used to be this complicated."

Jane patted him and nudged him back. She slid off the counter. "Let me go, and we'll be over there after a while."

"Have I said I don't want to do this?"

"Yes, I think you have. Maybe after supper, Laura and MayLynn will find something to talk about other than Zachary, and you can show me your room."

Bo cracked a smile. "For all the good it would do me."

"I'm willing. You're the one withholding."

"How's that song go? Something about liking it enough to put a ring on it."

"I think that's my line. Quit stressing about it all. It will work out like it needs to." She caressed his blue-jeaned butt as they walked to the door. "I'll give you a half-hour head start. If you need longer, text me."

"I won't."

****

Bo stood inside the back door. It took everything in him not to take off his shoes. She was standing in the middle of the kitchen waiting for him. She must have heard his truck. "Hi, Mama."

"Hi. Where's Jane and Laura?"

"They'll be along. Jane thought it might be good for you and me to have some time together first."

"She's a very sweet girl." MayLynn looked more fragile than Bo remembered.

"Yes, she is." He'd never met a more giving and kind woman.

"Want some tea?"

"Sure."

She turned toward the counter intent on the task. Bo sat down at the table for a lack of anything better to do. When had it become awkward to be here? His mother brought the tea to him, handing him the glass.

Bo looked at his mother. Really looked at her. "Did Dad know?"

MayLynn sat at the table. "Yes. I was so young and stupid. I threw myself at Isaiah, thinking that your dad was cheating on me. And maybe he was. I always thought he was, though he swore he didn't. Isaiah was very kind. He'd lost his wife that year, and in a moment of weakness, he gave in. He knew it was a mistake, but I wouldn't let it go. And then your daddy found out. I thought he would be so angry, but he wasn't. He left that day, and when he came back, he told me that Isaiah was leaving. And I had a choice. I could go with him and never come back, or I could stay and try to put our marriage back together." Tears glittered in her eyes. "I chose to stay."

"Dad knew I might not be his."

"Oh, honey." MayLynn leaned forward and folded her hands on the table in front of her. "The second he saw you, you were his. I never saw a man so proud of a son in my life. His grin was from ear to ear in the delivery room. Even though he was working and I wasn't, he'd get up at night when you cried. He loved you so much. I wish none of it had happened, in a sense, but in another way, I'm glad it did, because, Bo, it made me realize what I almost lost. It showed me the kind of man Zachary was. His character, that he could love me in spite of what I had done, and from then on I started trying to be the wife he deserved."

They sat there for a few moments as Bo digested what she had said.

"Is there anything else you want to know?"

MayLynn's face was calm, but watchful.

"Thank you for telling me all of this, and thank you for inviting Laura over here. That means a lot to Jane, and it means a lot to me."

"You really like Jane."

"I think I want to marry her." As he said the words, Bo realized they were true.

"You haven't known her for very long." She said it in a neutral tone, as if she were making an observation instead of a judgment.

"I know her heart. Family means everything to her. I think that's a good quality in a wife. Plus, she seems to fit in here well." She absolutely did. Happiness spread through him.

"I like her a lot better than Amber. Amber is nice enough, but you'd always take a backseat to the diner."

"Plus, she's a better cook than you."

MayLynn's glared at him. "She is not." She scooted her chair back and walked over to the oven. She bent down and looked in the window.

"Okay, she's not."

Taking a fork from the counter, she opened the oven door and reached inside briefly then examined the tines of the fork. Placing it back on the counter, she put on oven mitts and pulled a round dish out of the oven and placed it on the stovetop.

"Want me to set the table?"

"Thank you. I already did."

"So, we're eating in the dining room?"

"Of course, we are. We're having company. You don't entertain guests in the kitchen." MayLynn put the mitts away. "Did you feed them in the kitchen before?" she said in an irritated tone.

"Yes."

"Son, I know I taught you better than that."

"Sorry." Bo decided it was wiser to apologize rather than remind her she had refused to come to dinner previously because she didn't want Laura in the house. In just a short time, a lot of progress had been made. Maybe purging their past history had helped to bring about the change in MayLynn's attitude.

He hoped.

The doorbell rang.

MayLynn reached behind her and untied her apron. She put it away. "Let's go greet our guests." Without waiting for a response, she walked out of the kitchen toward the front of the house, and Bo followed her.

Opening the door, MayLynn stepped back.

Laura stood on the porch with Jane behind her. The difference in Laura since Bo had seen her the last time caught him unaware. Her face looked thinner, and her skin had a sickly pallor to it. Bo's attention turned to Jane. Surely, she had noticed Laura didn't look good.

"Come in. Come in," MayLynn said. "Laura, how are you?"

Laura walked into the house. "I've been better."

"Oh?" MayLynn asked as she led them into the sitting room. Bo followed the two older women and caught Jane's hand in his as he fell into step next to her.

"I think I was long overdue for a vacation. All I seem to want to do is lay around."

"What kind of work do you do?" MayLynn asked.

Jane's hand felt warm. He tightened his fingers around hers.

"How did it go?" she murmured.

"Good."

Jane smiled up at him. "I'm glad."

Dinner went off without a hitch. MayLynn was warm and friendly, and Bo could tell she was making an extra effort to make Laura and Jane feel welcome. Not long after they had moved to the sitting room, Jane spoke.

"Would you forgive us if we leave now? Laura usually doesn't get out at night, and I can tell she's tired."

"I'll be tired whether I'm here or at the house," Laura replied.

"Yes, but at the house you can go lie down."

"Have you seen a doctor, Laura?" MayLynn asked.

"She refuses to go," Jane said.

"I bet that makes Jane worry," Bo said.

Laura made an irritated sound. "Don't you start. They'll just want to run a bunch of tests and take up a whole bunch of my time."

"What else do you have to do?" Jane asked in that gentle way of hers. "You have the summer off from work. This is a good opportunity to get a thorough check-up so they can figure out why you're so tired all the time."

Laura stood up. "MayLynn, you've been wonderful. Everything tasted great, and your house is beautiful, as I knew it would be."

"You never have been in the house before, have you?"

Laura gazed steadily at the other woman. "No," she said quietly.

MayLynn walked over to her. "I'm sorry for how I acted, Laura."

"Ah, that was a long time ago. I don't blame you for being jealous. Zachary was a good catch, and you were afraid he hadn't stayed caught. He did, though. He was like a brother to me. I'm sorry he died so young."

"Thank you."

Laura glanced back at Jane. "I think I will take you up on your offer to go home, Jane."

Bo and Jane were sitting next to each other on the couch holding hands. Bo leaned over and kissed her briefly. "Can I come over later?"

"I'd like that."

After Jane and Laura left, Bo helped MayLynn put the food away and clean up. When all the chores were done, MayLynn wiped her hands on a dish towel. "Would you go in the sitting room? I want to show you something."

"All right."

"Give me a few minutes to get it," she said, walking out of the kitchen.

Puzzled, Bo refilled his tea glass and went and sat down as directed. In a few moments, MayLynn came in with an old jewelry box.

"This was your grandmother's jewelry box—Grandma Anderson, your daddy's mother."

Bo caught the slight emphasis on *your*. MayLynn sat down beside him on the couch with the box in her lap. She pushed the small brass button on the front and the top opened. She lifted the lid. "You can have all of this now. Maybe there is something that Jane would like?"

What?

"You want to give some of Grandma's jewelry to Jane?"

"If you're thinking about marrying her, then it might be nice to give her something from your family." MayLynn lifted a chain with a small silver angel with a blue trinket in its middle. "Your dad and I gave this to her after you were born. This is your birthstone. Do you think she would like that?"

"I don't know."

She handed the necklace to him. "I think silver would look pretty on her with her dark hair." She pulled out a small box. "This is what I was looking for." Opening the lid, she pulled out a diamond ring in a silver antique setting and a matching silver wedding band. "This was Grandma's engagement ring and wedding ring. If you decide to ask her to marry you, you could use this as the engagement ring."

She held the rings in her open palm for his inspection. Bo's heart thumped heavy in his chest. All of this seemed surreal. He reached over and picked up the rings, sliding them on his pinkie finger to his knuckle where they settled. He gazed at them.

"Mom, you surprise me. Are you really okay with me marrying Jane?"

MayLynn nodded. "If you love her, and if you think she's the one, then of course I'm okay with it. And like I said, I like her a lot better than Amber. Amber is just a little too sarcastic for my taste. Jane is kind, and she respects her elders. She also loves my flowers. I like that about her."

She sorted through the jewelry in the box. "Oh, these are pretty. Does she have pierced ears?"

Bo remembered running his tongue over tiny diamond studs in her ear lobe. "Yes."

"They're opals. Some people won't wear them if they're not their birthstone, but I don't believe in that superstition. She might though. Do you know her birthday?"

"No."

"Do you think she wants children?"

Bo burst out laughing.

MayLynn looked at him with a troubled expression. "What? She doesn't like children?"

"She likes kids. She wants kids."

"Kids? She wants a big family?"

"Yes, I think because she grew up in foster care. She never had a family before she married Laura's son." Bo smiled at the ring that twinkled in the light. He was warming up to the idea of having a baby with Jane. *Yeah*. He could see himself doing that.

"When are you getting married?"

The question stopped Bo short. "I just said I was thinking about asking her. I didn't say I was definitely going to do it."

"Well, okay. If you decide to do it, do you think a spring wedding?"

"No. We plant in the spring. Have to be the winter when things aren't so busy." He handed the rings back to her. "But I haven't decided yet."

MayLynn's mouth opened in a wide grin. "You've already decided. Otherwise, you wouldn't have thought about the wedding needing to be in the winter."

He stood up. "It's common sense, Mom."

"Here," she said closing the box and handing it to him. "Take this. When you decide you've decided, you can use the ring if you want. Or anything else in there you like, you can give to her to butter her up for saying 'yes'."

"She'll say yes." Bo tucked the box into his side.

"Why are you so sure?"

"'Cause I'm a good catch, that's why."

And she wants to have my baby. But Bo wasn't going tell his mama that.

Chapter Sixteen

By the time Bo went over to their house, Jane was sitting on the front steps leaning against the tree. She'd changed into shorts and a white T-shirt and taken off her shoes. She looked beautiful with her hair down all around her shoulders.

"Hey," he said. "Laura okay?"

Jane shrugged. "She went to bed a little while ago. I wish I could talk her into going to the doctor." Her brown eyes looked at him as he stood on the bottom step. "Something is really wrong, and she won't talk about it. She won't let me do anything about it."

Bo put his hand out, and she took it. He gently pulled her to her feet, sat down on the spot she'd vacated, and then settled her on his lap. She was warm and soft next to him, and he nuzzled her hair.

"Just take her to the doctor. Tell her you're going to get ice cream or something."

Jane turned her face to glance back at him. "Would your mother let you take her to the doctor against her will?"

"Well, I could probably make her do it, but it wouldn't be fun, I tell you that. I'd probably need a few beers afterward."

"Laura is stubborn. If she doesn't want to do something, I've never been ever able to strong arm her into doing it. The best I've been able to do is wear her down by gentle nudges. But I think I'm running out of time. If it's something serious, she needs to go now so we can actually do something about it."

"Tell you what. I'll come by around eight in the morning, and we'll take her to the urgent care place over in Athens. I'll get Jonathan to meet us over there, and then I'll come back with him. You think that would work?" Bo slid his arms around her middle and hugged her to him. He rested his chin on her shoulder.

"I hope so. It's just not like her to be so tired all the time. Did you notice she barely ate anything tonight?"

"Yes, I noticed."

Jane moved her hand to his and interlaced her fingers with his. "Want to come inside?"

"Sure. What did you have in mind?"

"We could turn the television on and neck on the couch."

"I like the way you think."

****

Early the next morning, Jane walked over to the barn. Bo exited the door just as she was ascending the stairs.

"Hi," he said. "I didn't expect to see you this morning. Want some coffee?"

"Yes," she said tersely.

He turned and opened the door and walked inside. He looked over his shoulder at her. "What's wrong?"

"She said she's not going to the doctor."

"When did you talk to her? Did she wake up after I left last night?"

"This morning. I heard her in the bathroom. I think she was throwing up. We just had a big fight about her going to get checked out."

"You had a fight with her? I would like to have seen that."

"I told her we were taking her to the hospital, and yes, she was going. And she said no, she wasn't, and I couldn't make her. And then she slammed the bedroom door and told me to leave her alone."

"Ah, let her cool off." He poured some coffee from the coffeemaker into a cup then fixed it the way she liked it. "Come on. We'll watch the sun rise on Hesed Rock."

On the rock, they sat side by side.

"Quit worrying about it. We'll work on her together and wear her down. We'll get her to the doctor."

"It's hard not to worry about it."

Bo leaned toward her, took her face in his hands, and gave her a slow, sweet kiss.

"Are you trying to distract me?" she asked.

"Yeah. Is it working?"

Jane leaned back and pulled her with him. "Not quite. Want to try harder?"

Bo wrapped his arm around her shoulders to pillow her head as she lay down on the rock. The mouths melded together and quickly everything went out of Jane's mind, but how good it felt to have Bo surrounding her. She tugged at his shirt, moving it up and out of the way so she could run her hands over his stomach and his chest. He grabbed it and pulled it over his head, then bunched it up under his head and positioned her on top of him. Jane leaned over him, her hair curtaining her face before she was close enough to kiss his skin.

"Do you think it would be awful to get naked on this rock?" Bo asked.

Jane grinned wickedly at him before sitting up and shedding her own shirt. "Depends on if I get to be on top or not."

"I will be on the bottom if you'll do me this one thing." He reached into his pocket and floundered a little bit trying to get his fingers fully into the material.

"What are you doing?"

He pulled his hand out and sat up, fisting his hand and holding it in between them. "I'd like you to wear this." He opened his hand, and a ring sat in the middle of his palm.

"Oh, Bo. How pretty." Jane plucked up the ring and put it on her hand. She looked at it on her finger. "It's gorgeous."

"No. Other hand." He slid the ring off her finger and held her left hand and slipped it on her ring finger. "Jane Stanford, would you do me the honor of marrying me and letting me give you those kids you want so bad?"

Jane's mouth fell open. "Oh, my gosh. Are you sure?"

"I'll probably be more sure if you take off your bra."

Jane laughed and reached behind her to unclasp the

undergarment. "What if somebody comes out here?"

"As long as you've been meeting me out here, how many people have you seen other than me and you?"

"No one." She slid her bra down her arms.

Bo pulled her on his lap and kissed her, and Jane lost her breath when her breasts pressed against his bare chest. Jane kneaded the muscles of his shoulder, enjoying the breadth of him, remembering again what it felt like to be this close to another person.

"Promise me something," Bo whispered as he tucked his fingers under the waistband of her jeans.

"What?"

"You'll marry me before you have a baby. You'll marry me even if we never have a baby. You'll marry me no matter what." He covered her breast with his other hand as if he were punctuating the statement.

"I'll marry you no matter what." She reached down and unbuttoned his pants, then slid the zipper down. She bent down and kissed his stomach, touching him through the denim. Kneeling on the rock, she pulled off the rest of her clothes until the only item she wore was the ring Bo had slipped on her finger.

As the sun broke over the tree line, they made love on the rock called Hesed. And when they were sated, Bo cradled her in his arms and whispered three words against the top of her hair.

"I love you."

Later Bo drove Jane over to the house to convince Laura that, yes, she was going to the urgent care place, and, no, they weren't going to take no for an answer.

They held hands up the stairs and beside the tree. Jane opened the door. The couch was empty, and the bathroom door stood open. Laura must have been in her bedroom.

"Is there a lock on the door?" Bo asked.

"Fortunately, no." Jane walked across the room and knocked softly. "Laura?" She opened the door and walked in.

Laura was in bed, covered with the blanket she carried

with her from bed to couch and back.

Her face was turned away from the door.

"Laura?" Jane sat on the bed and put her hand on the woman's shoulder, shaking her lightly. She didn't respond. Jane leaned forward to peer at her face, and saw the ashy color of the woman's skin, and....

"Laura! Bo! Bo! Something's wrong with Laura. We need to get her to the hospital."

****

In the few seconds it took Bo to get in the room, Jane had her fingers next to Laura's neck. "She's got a pulse, but it's erratic. Call 911."

Bo didn't move. Flashes of the day four years ago pierced his mind. Zachary's skin had the same dead pale color as Laura's.

Bo had seen the tractor in the field, the engine still running and his dad slumped in the seat.

"Dad!" he'd yelled, opening the door and catching his dad as he fell into his arms. "No, Dad. Dad!" Bo had dragged him out of the tractor and laid him on the dirt in between a row of beans. "Dad, please," he'd whimpered. But the man was gone. Cold already.

"Bo."

Jane's voice propelled him to the present.

Jane looked at him, her expression determined. "Bo, call 911 now." Her tone was sharp and clipped.

Bo unhooked his phone from his belt and did as Jane told him.

"Laura? Laura!" Jane said to her. "Come on." She bent down and patted her cheek. "Wake up."

"Where's the closest emergency room?" she asked, rubbing her neck, then her face.

"Forty minutes."

"How quick can they get an ambulance here?"

"Fifteen. Maybe twenty minutes."

"Can they get a life flight here quicker?"

Bo asked the 911 operator.

"Tell them we'll meet them at the highway. It's flat

there with no trees or power lines," Jane said. Bo relayed the information. She pointed to the phone. "Give me the phone. You carry Laura to your truck. Let's go."

In twelve minutes, a helicopter had landed at the designated location, and two emergency technicians in life flight suits had Laura on a gurney and were working on her. Laura had gained consciousness and her color improved. As soon as she was in the 'copter and it had lifted off the ground, Jane headed to the truck. "Take me to the house. I'll get the car and drive to the hospital."

"Let me drive you."

"It makes more sense for me to drive myself. That way you can go to work, and I won't be stuck at the hospital without a way to get around." She closed the truck door.

Bo got in on the driver's side and cranked the engine. Admiration filled his chest, but it was tempered with frustration for how calm and distant she appeared.

"Jane, you don't have to do this alone. I want to be with you. I want to be here for you."

She blinked rapidly and lifted her hand to swipe her eye. "I can't lose her, Bo."

He reached over and took her fingers. "We'll go by the house, and you can get some clothes in case you want to stay the night."

"I'm not leaving her."

"All right. We'll go together."

****

By the time they arrived at the hospital, Laura was in surgery. The doctor who met with them said her heart wasn't working as it should and probably hadn't been for a while. He cautioned Jane that Laura had to be intubated, but if she responded well to treatment, she ought to be breathing on her own within a few days post-surgery.

Bo stayed at Jane's side in the waiting room.

"Want to get something to eat?" he asked.

She shook her head. "Why don't you go back to Haven? I'll be okay."

Bo frowned. "Stop this."

"Stop what?"

"Stop acting like I'm not part of this."

Jane shook her head in confusion. "What do you mean?"

Bo raised her hand and kissed the ring on her finger. "You've got me. Use me. Lean on me. That's what I'm here for."

"She's all I've had for a long time. I'm not used to leaning on anyone else."

"Isn't it a good thing you have someone to lean on now? Now come on." He pulled her to her feet. "We worked up an appetite this morning on the rock before all of this happened, and I'm famished."

"I shouldn't have..." She pulled her hand away. "If I had stayed with her, this wouldn't have happened."

"Yes, it would have happened. In fact, if you had been asleep this morning, it's possible it would have been much later that you found her."

Bo didn't say it, but he was implying she would have died. But Jane couldn't let go of the guilt haranguing her.

"I would have been there. I should have made her go to the doctor weeks ago."

"Yeah? And how were you going to do that? She refused to go. You told me that yourself. Now, let me be a good husband here and feed you so you don't get sick as well."

"We're not married."

"We're not married yet, but I don't like that word fiancé. It sounds...." He shrugged.

"Presumptuous?"

He shot her an irritated look. "Highfalutin'. Let's go eat."

"What if she gets out of surgery?"

"Then we'll tell the lady at the desk that we'll be down in the cafeteria and to call us." He walked up to a woman sitting at a desk in the corner. She wore a red vest signifying she worked for the hospital. "We're with Laura Stanford. We're going to get some lunch. Would you call us if she gets out of surgery before we get back?"

"Certainly. Just write your cell number right here." She turned a paper around on the desk and handed him a pen. He bent down and wrote on the paper. When he straightened, he held out his hand to Jane.

"All right?"

Jane sighed in defeat and allowed him to lead her through the waiting room door toward the cafeteria.

Laura was taken to the intensive care unit after surgery. Jane wasn't allowed to see her until several hours later because of the restrictive visitation hours. Bo's calming presence kept Jane's anxiety at bay, and by late that afternoon, she was at Laura's bedside. Though she had a ventilator tube coming out of her mouth, her skin color looked better than it had in a long time. The doctor was optimistic about her prognosis, and when Jane walked out of the unit, her legs wobbled in relief. Bo stood in the hallway waiting for her. He must have noticed her shakiness because he put his arm around her shoulders.

"You all right?" he said as they walked down the hallway toward the ICU waiting room.

"Yes. Yes. The doctor says he thinks she's going to be okay. She might be in a regular room by the end of the week."

"What about you?"

"I'm all right."

"How about I drive us home, and we'll come back first thing in the morning?"

Jane shook her head. "I'm not leaving her."

"Okay."

"But you go on. I'll call you tomorrow."

"You sure are trying hard to get rid of me."

"I'm not, but I just know you've got a farm to run."

"And I have a woman to take care of."

"I can take care of her."

"I'm talking about you."

Joy erupted in Jane's heart. It did feel good to have someone to lean on. She gave his shoulder a little nuzzle.

"It is nice to have a fiancé, I suppose."

"I don't like that word. Let's just get married now so we don't have to use it."

"I'm not getting married until Laura is out of the woods."

"It sounds like the doctor thinks she'll be out of the woods by the end of the week. We'll have something to celebrate."

"I hope so."

That night she and Bo slept on reclining chairs side-by-side in the family waiting room. The next morning, while they were eating breakfast in the cafeteria, MayLynn walked up to their table. Jane looked at her in surprise. Bo leaned over and kissed Jane. "Mom's going to stay with you today. I'll be back tonight. All right?"

Jane, overcome with emotion, could only nod her head.

He stood up. "I'll call you later." He squeezed MayLynn's shoulder affectionately. "Thanks, Mama."

****

"I don't want to stay here," Laura declared. Bo and Jane were on either side of her walking her into MayLynn's house.

"Yes, we know," Jane said.

MayLynn stood holding the door open. "It's just for a little while. Until you're stronger."

"I'm stronger now."

"Think of it as an extended pajama party," MayLynn suggested.

"Oh, give me a break," Laura said angrily.

"Laura, until Miles gets all those windows in and finishes the floor, this is the better option," Jane counseled. "You don't need to be around all that construction dust."

"Great. Is this how it's going to be? I've got three people bossing me around now."

"It's better than all of the nurses at the hospital, isn't it?" Jane guided her toward the staircase. She could tell Bo was supporting some of the woman's weight.

"I only had one of them at a time, and they didn't hover."

"Can you make it up the stairs, Laura?" MayLynn asked.

"I can carry her."

"You try it, buster, and I'll club you."

They stepped onto the first stair. "She's very grumpy since she got discharged. Does she have a pill for that, Jane?"

MayLynn led the procession. She shot a harsh look over her shoulder at her son, speaking his name in a chastising tone.

"Yeah, Bo. Quit talking about me like I'm not here."

Bo smiled. He kind of liked getting fussed at by two old women but thought better of saying it aloud.

****

Bo lounged on the couch and patted the cushion next to him when Jane walked in the room.

"How's she doing?"

"Okay. I think the trip tired her out." Jane settled next to him on the couch.

Bo wrapped his arms around her and pulled her to him. He began to nibble on her neck.

Jane resisted. "What if your mother walks in?"

"Then my hope is she will walk right back out." He pulled at her shirt and snaked his hand underneath. "After two weeks of sleeping in hospital waiting rooms, it's going to be so good to sleep in a bed. With you."

"I don't know. I might better stay with Laura in her room."

"She's right. You do hover." Bo brushed her hair away from her face and rained kisses across her cheek until he reached her mouth, then he touched his lips to hers.

Jane sighed in pleasure and lay back on the couch, returning his affection. A noise from the door alerted her MayLynn had indeed come into the room. They sat up, and Jane straightened her shirt.

"Excuse me." MayLynn's attention was on the back

wall. "Jane, I was going to ask you which bedroom you wanted, but perhaps you already know."

"We were just talking about that."

"Yeah, she needs to sleep in my room, so Laura can get her rest."

"Whatever you want to do is okay with me. I'm going upstairs if you need anything."

Bo began pulling Jane on his lap. "'Night, Mom."

"Can you at least wait until she's out the door?" Jane hissed.

MayLynn's footsteps sounded on the stairs.

"See? She's already gone."

"I think we need to talk."

Bo groaned. "Okay." He lay down and positioned her in between his body and the back of the couch. He grinned down at her. "What are we going to talk about?"

"Getting married."

"Finally giving in, are you?" He kissed the tip of her nose. "Let's get married the day of the Harvest party."

Jane's eyes widened. "That's in three weeks."

"Yep. We can get married, and then the Harvest party could be our reception. We can have the ceremony on the back patio. It'll be real nice."

"I think we ought to get married in the church. I didn't get to have a church wedding with Mandy, and I think it would be nice to have a religious ceremony."

"You think the Lord can't be a part of the wedding on the back patio?"

"You know what I mean, don't you? We have a lot to be thankful for, and I think it's an appropriate way to begin our marriage."

"All right. Wedding at the church. Reception here at the Harvest party. That means it will have to be a morning wedding. Are you okay with that?"

"In three weeks?"

"Life is precarious." Bo's gaze moved lovingly over Jane's face. "I think there's something to be said about not planning too far ahead, because if you do, sometimes those things don't get to happen. Some wise woman told me that, and spending all that time in the ICU waiting room made me think she knew what the heck she was talking about."

Love for this man filled Jane's chest. "I love you. You make me so happy. I can't believe you went back and forth every day to the hospital just to be with us."

Bo's eyes widened as he remembered that day. "I can't believe how calm you were when Laura was as sick as she was. I could barely think straight."

"I didn't do anything but take her pulse, try to get her to wake up, and tell you to call 911."

"You were amazing."

"Thanks. After the wedding, I don't want to leave Laura." Jane studied his expression carefully. "Are you going to be okay living there with us?"

"You want us to live in that itty-bitty house?" he said in disbelief.

"I don't like her being alone, especially as sick as she has been, and I don't think she'll be happy anywhere else."

"All right," Bo said.

"Really?"

"It's not ideal, but, Jane, if that's where you want to be, then I want to be there with you. Where you go, I will go. And where you stay, I will stay."

"Where did you hear that?" Jane asked.

"I heard you say it to Laura one time. I think later, especially if we have a bunch of kids, we'll have to figure something else out, but right now we'll do that."

"We could live in your apartment," she suggested.

"It's kind of small for a family too. Besides, if we move out there, people will start coming out there bugging us. I like it private. That way if I want to make love to you on the rock, I can without worrying about being interrupted."

"Would you want to live here?"

"With my mom? You'd want to live with my mom?" Bo asked in astonishment.

"It's a big house, and you live here already when you're not at your apartment. And it seems like your mom would be so lonely here. How do you think she'd feel about us living here?"

Bo raised his arm in a gesture of surrender. "She'd love it."

"All right."

"Well, it's settled then."

"Good. Let's go to bed." He locked his arm around her, swung her around his body, and sat up. Then he jumped off the couch and pulled her to her feet.

"It's barely nine o'clock."

"I get up at five. That only gives me a little less than eight hours to be in the bed with you."

Epilogue

The little boy reached forward and ran his fingers across the carving in the tree. "Grandma? How come Daddy cut these letters in the skin of your tree?"

Laura studied the trunk of the tree. "He was telling your mama and anybody else who saw it that he loved her. See the heart?"

"Yeah. Seems kind of mean to do to the tree."

"It didn't hurt the tree any. It still grew. The stairs used to be around the tree, but the tree kept growing so finally your daddy had Miles move the door of the house and put the stairs down a ways next to the tree. That's the thing about love and trees. They just keep growing." Laura put her hand in the boy's head and mussed his hair. "A lot like you."

"Yeah. I used to not be able to touch the letters. Now I can. When's Mama and Daddy getting back?"

"Don't you like spending the night with me, Ben?" Laura asked.

"Yeah." His blue eyes—so much like his daddy's—gazed sadly at his grandma. "But I don't know why they couldn't take me with them to the barn."

"Because I wanted you to stay here with me. If you don't come out here every once in a while, who am I going to eat s'mores with or play Go Fish?"

"Yeah. Hope is too little to do those things with you." Ben mentioned his sister who was only eighteen months old. "And when the new baby comes, this may be the only place to get peace and quiet."

"A big family's nice, Ben." She smiled down at him. "And since you're the oldest, you get to boss the little ones around."

"I hope Mama has a boy," he said in a somber tone.

"Maybe she will."

"What do you think they do out there at the barn without me and Hope?"

"Well, mostly they let me and your other grandmother have you all to ourselves. Your Grandmother MayLynn gets Hope, and I get you. Then the next time, we switch it around."

"What about when the new baby comes?"

"We'll work something out. You're not worried about it, are you?"

"I like being the only one out here. Hope is always trying to get my toys, and we can't play Go Fish with her around."

The sound of a truck engine alerted them that Bo and Jane were returning.

"Oh, it's Mom and Dad. All right!"

"I figured they'd be back pretty soon after breakfast. They like to watch the sun rise out there. Your mama said she was sitting on that rock the first time she ever saw your daddy."

"I don't know what they think is so special about that big old rock."

"I imagine it's who they're with that makes it special."

The End

Wait. Don't stop reading yet. Keep going, and you will find:

*Author's Note – Reflecting on the story this book is based on.

*My book *Faithful*, or at least, the first chapter of it. I love this story, and I think you will, too.

AUTHOR'S NOTE

"Now Naomi had a relative...a man of standing, whose name was Boaz."
Ruth 2:1

I consider Boaz, the male lead of Ruth, a book in the Old Testament, the most romantic hero I've ever read. What a shame this beautiful story isn't more well known, though you may have heard the famous quotation from the book. "Where you go, I will go, where you stay, I will stay. Your people will be my people, and your God, my God" (Ruth 1:16).

You've probably heard these lines recited at a wedding ceremony where two people pledge their life-long love to each other. But in the context of this book, it is said by a young widow to her widowed mother-in-law. It expresses the bond she feels with this woman, though she is no longer tied to her through marriage. It always strikes me as odd it has become synonymous with the marriage bond between a man and a woman when the connection is really about commitment of family that even death cannot break. If one wants to be true to the Biblical context, then the young bride ought to recite this to her groom's mother, and I can't see anyone agreeing to that!

Even though the book is called Ruth, the story begins with Naomi, her husband, and two sons who leave their homeland to go to Moab. There the sons marry Moabite women, one of whom is Ruth. When all the men in the family die, Naomi decides to go back home a broken-hearted woman. Her pain is so deep, she calls herself "Mara" which means "bitter."

Ruth—whose name sounds like the Hebrew word for friendship—accompanies the bitter and broken woman back home—two widows who have nothing but each other. It's a very sad beginning. But we find Naomi does have a few things going for her: a relative named Boaz and a little plot of land. Almost from the beginning, we see Boaz's kindness as he allows Ruth to glean from his fields and makes sure none of his field hands bother her (Ruth 2: 8-9, 3: 15-16). He's moved to do this because he's heard about how faithful she has been to Naomi (2:11). Even though his mother isn't in the story, I imagine Boaz was the type of man who loved his mama because he is so touched by how Ruth treats Naomi.

The threshing floor scene in chapter three is perhaps the most sensuous scene in the whole Bible. Basically, Naomi dolls Ruth up to convince Boaz to have sex with her so she can conceive. This is because the Levirate Law states if a woman is widowed before she has a child, the closest male relative of the husband is to impregnate the widow. The baby—hopefully, a son, since we are dealing with a patriarchal society—will be considered the dead husband's offspring. In the book of Ruth, they call the man, whose role this is, the "kinsman-redeemer," and it explains several things that happen in the story, such as why Ruth wants to lie down with Boaz and why Boaz seeks out the unnamed man who is actually a closer relative.

We see Boaz's gentlemanly character here. Even though it may be he has passed out from drinking too much (Ruth 3:7); nevertheless, he does not take advantage of Ruth when she "uncovers his feet" (3:7). In the Hebrew, the word for "feet" can also mean "genitalia" and since Ruth is actually seeking a man to give her a baby, I think you can make a case that she's actually not uncovering his feet at all—but another part of him. If this is true, then can you imagine the kind of man Boaz was not to take what this young woman offered? Not only that, but he makes sure no one sees her leave and he gives her food to take back to Naomi. His gentlemanly behavior just makes me swoon.

The rural setting seemed fitting to the story I called *Steadfast*, so I kept that. And even though Bo isn't on the threshing floor when Jane goes to him, the rock and his apartment in the barn feel close enough. And what about this rock called Hesed? Hesed means "steadfast" or "loving kindness" in English. In Ruth 3:10, Boaz uses this word when he responds to Ruth's uncovering of his feet and her appeal to "cover me with your garment." I don't know why I thought the great big rock in the field was such a good symbol of loving kindness. Maybe because it is permanent, and it would be strong enough to bear the weight of two families becoming one family. I also loved that the rock didn't seem to belong in the field, but yet there it was.

In Scripture, Ruth is a Moabite, a foreigner, and yet she demonstrates a faithfulness, a loyalty that was an inspiration to the Israelite people. Through her, Naomi has her grandson, and perhaps a healing from all the loss she suffered. The book of Ruth begins and ends with Naomi. In the end, she has a future through her grandson, Ruth's son. That's why I chose to end my book with Laura and her grandson, to express the happily ever after, not only for Bo and Jane, but for Laura as well.

Ruth is important enough as a Biblical character that she is mentioned in the genealogy of Jesus Christ. And Boaz's character is so compelling that his story trumps the Levirate Law, and he—instead of Ruth's dead husband—is named as the father of Ruth's child in the Gospel of Matthew (1:5). The Hesed—the loving kindness—of both Ruth and Boaz—deserve a place in the most romantic couples of all time. I hope you enjoyed my effort to modernize their story here.

****

If you enjoyed this adaptation of the Biblical story, I hope you will look for *Faithful*, my retelling of the Genesis hero Jacob and the two sisters who loved him and *Tomorrow's Child*, my retelling of an amazing and brave woman named Tamara. All three of these books make up my series known as "Family Tangles: A New Spin on Some Ancient Tales".

And if you love heroes who are a little broken, my book, *Shadow of a Scent*, is available in print and at digital retailers.

Following is the beginning of my book *Faithful*. I hope you enjoy it enough to want to keep reading and buy it.

Faithful

Chapter One

"What do you think about having Noel's baby?"

Nila stared at her twin waiting for the punch line, examining the face so much like her own for a hint of mirth. Nothing.

"I think it would be weird since he's your husband." Noel also happened to be Nila's best guy friend and her brother-in-law.

"I need you to get over the weirdness, Nila. Dr. Garber has scheduled me for a hysterectomy next month."

"Lil! Why didn't you tell me?"

Lil had never been on birth control in the seven years she and Noel had been married. In the last year, they had been trying in earnest to conceive with no success. When Lil began having severe abdominal pain, she had gone to see her OB/GYN.

"I am telling you."

"Is it…?" Nila couldn't make herself say the word.

Lil gazed out the window, tears filling her eyes.

"Lil!"

"No."

"Lil, please. It's not…?" Nila begged.

"It's just a uterine tumor."

"Just a uterine tumor? *Just* a uterine tumor? Does Noel know?"

"Not yet."

"Geez, Lil!"

"It would be a good idea for you to get checked out though. As soon as you can, just in case."

Lil stood up and walked over to the counter pulling a tissue out of its decorative box and touching it to the corner of each eye. She sniffed and glanced up at the ceiling. Nila studied the woman.

"Are you sure it isn't cancer?" Finally, Nila pushed that word past her lips, the disease that had killed their mother after she had suffered round after round of chemotherapy. "I mean, a tumor usually means cancer. Right?"

"They're going to run a few tests, but the doctor says the shape of the tumor indicates it is fibroid and non-cancerous. The surgery will take care of it." She squared her shoulders and sniffed again. "But not the problem of

Junior." Sitting back down across from her sister, she grasped her hands. "I can't have him now, so I need you to do it for me."

"You guys are on the adoption list, Lil. You should give it time."

Lil snorted. "Three years on the off chance we'll be approved?"

"Well, it's not the end of the world if you can't have kids. Lots of people don't have kids, and they do fine."

"But we want kids. We really want them. Noel..." Lil gave a watery laugh. "Noel opened a college account. Did I tell you? He's determined the baby's going to UK."

The back door opened, and Noel walked in. When he saw the two women, he stopped. Looking from one to the other, his expression turned to stone. Nila sat back as the charged air shot back and forth between husband and wife.

"Oh, Noel!" Lil sobbed. He was across the room within a second, and she launched herself into his arms.

Noel held her head to his chest and buried his face in her hair. Anguish ripped at Nila's heart. She shoved her chair back, picked up her purse, and walked out of the house not wanting to impose on this private moment between Lil and Noel.

By the time she got to her car, Nila's breaths were coming in short gasps. She sat in her car working to unclench her teeth. She beat on the steering wheel a few times.

It should have been me. My uterus with the damn tumor in it!

What did she need her uterus for anyway? It's not like any man would ever want to have a baby with her.

****

The purple sky indicated the impending appearance of the sun. Nila sat on the ground at the park with legs outstretched warming up for her morning run. She expected Noel to join her any minute because they had a standing running date three days a week. The triangulated relationship among the three of them had been ironed out years ago when Nila moved back to Cedarton a few years after Lil and Noel married. Nila and Lil kept their sisterly bond when Noel was absent. Nila and Noel hung out without Lil. And Nila always made herself scarce when Noel and Lil were together. There was nothing more pathetic than being the third wheel.

Heavy footsteps approached, their staccato beat announcing Noel's arrival. He and Lil lived less than a mile from here, so he ran instead of driving.

"Come on, slow poke, or I'll leave you in the dust."

"We'll see about that, Dearing." Nila shot from the ground and took off in a sprint.

In seconds, he caught up with her, and she slowed as they matched their rhythm and speed. One lap around with no words.

"You okay?"

"Sure."

"Really okay with all of this?"

"She's got to have the surgery. Of course, I'm okay with it. We'll try to adopt. If we can't…" He didn't finish.

"If you can't?"

"We won't have kids."

"Lil is talking about artificial insemination."

"No extraordinary measures, and besides, it's not fair to you."

"Who says I'll be the surrogate?"

Noel grinned at her. "Yours will be the only available uterus, Sister. What? You think we'd just open up the yellow pages under *Surrogate Mothers*?"

How ridiculous would that be? Nila knew in ancient times women had babies for other women, but it wasn't so common now. What did they call those women? Handmaids, maybe. She wiped the sweat off her brow with her forearm. "How far we going today?"

"Eight miles?"

Nila suppressed her grimace and nodded instead.

"I was thinking of getting her a dog. Maybe it'll get her mind off obsessing about a kid."

Nila cast him a disparaging glance. "Right. Kids. Dogs. Same difference."

****

Yours will be the only available uterus.

Nila sliced through the cardboard with a box cutter and lifted the lid revealing soccer shoe boxes. Could she really carry Noel and Lil's baby for them then give it up?

She sorted the boxes by shoe size before placing them neatly on the storage shelf. As owner of *Play It! Sports*, Cedarton's only dedicated sporting goods store, Nila could unpack inventory flawlessly while working through a problem. She had bought the store from the previous owner using some of the insurance money from her mom's death. The success of the store demonstrated her passion for sports and her good business sense in the three years of her ownership.

She had thought about having her own family from time to time instead of horning in on Noel and Lil. She had been out with a few men here and there, but nothing had ever come from any of it. Lil had been the one to have boyfriends; Nila had been the one to be a friend to boys.

As twin sisters, they had always been close. A long ago memory surfaced in Nila's mind. They had been five years old when the wreck happened. Lil lay in the hospital bed in the pediatric intensive care unit, breathing with the benefit of a ventilator. Nila sat on her mom's lap.

Nila cast a troubled gaze at her twin. "Mama? Is Lila going to be okay?"

"I hope so, sweetie. She inhaled a lot of smoke in the accident, and the doctor says it hurt her lungs."

Nila began to cry. "I'm scared."

Her mother wiped the tears from the little girl's cheeks. "You've got to be strong for your sissy, Nila. She's depending on us now to make sure she's okay."

"What if she dies like Daddy?"

Mom held Nila's hands in her own. The sadness and determination in them struck Nila even to this day. "Nila, darling. Lila is so very fragile right now. I don't know what's going to happen, but it's in God's hands. The best we can do is love her and take care of her. Okay?"

"I do love her, and I promise I will always take care of her, Mama. I'll take care of my sissy no matter what."

Nila had taken that promise to heart throughout the years. She had often put Lil's needs ahead of her own and done what she could to keep Lil from getting anxious because it often triggered her asthma.

But Lil was asking a lot.

Could Nila give up a baby she carried even if she was giving it to her own sister, knowing she would always be a fixture in the child's life? Not as Mommy, but as Aunt Nila?

Could she?

Nila sat back on her heels and imagined Noel's baby. His chocolate eyes. The endearing curly-blond hair. She didn't know much about genetics, but she hoped their baby would have his dad's good looks.

Their baby. Not her baby.

Nila shook her head. No. Lil was going to have to figure something else out. Noel had said no artificial insemination. His insistence they take no extraordinary measures would get her off the hook.

****

"Cool!" Benny Fitzgerald yelled when a six-foot geyser shot forth from a two-liter soda bottle.

Nila grinned at her eight-year-old neighbor. "Should we go for six candies?"

Nila slid the white mint nugget through a homemade funnel into the opening of the bottle then jumped back to avoid being spewed. The hard coating, reacting to the carbonation, created an impressive soda fountain and made a heck of a mess on her back deck.

"Wow!" Lil called as she boarded the stairs.

"Hey, Sis." Nila stood back with hands on hips surveying proudly the soda covered wood and half-empty bottles before noticing her sister's hands cuddled a small blanket to her chest. "What 'cha got?"

"My new baby. Come inside and let me show you."

Nila hid her surprise. Had Lil flipped? "I'll see you, Benny."

"Sure thing, Miss Nila. Can I come back tomorrow?"

"Yeah, dude, but you bring the pop. We went through all my bottles in less than eight minutes." She high-fived the boy before the women walked into the house, their childhood home and where Nila still lived.

Once inside, Lil uncovered the cutest kitten Nila had ever seen.

"Aww! Let me hold it."

"Isn't she precious? Lil handed the tabby over, and Nila cradled her close to her chest.

"You cute little thing," she crooned.

"Noel brought her home last night. Hey, listen. Have you made an appointment with Dr. Garber? He really wants to make sure you're okay since we're twins."

"No, I haven't gotten around to it."

"You need to. I'm not trying to be bossy, but—"

"But you are."

"Promise me. As soon as you can. Okay?"

"Okay, okay." They sat on the couch while Nila stroked the kitten's soft fur. "Have you named her?"

"I was thinking *Daisy*. What do you think?"

"Daisy's good. Daisy is a fine name for my little niece."

Lil gave her best *sister* gaze to Nila.

Uh oh.

"You know, Nila, I wouldn't mind if you made love to Noel, because if the result would be a real niece or nephew for you, that would be awesome."

Uneasiness filled Nila at the sincere expression on Lil's face. She did not want to disappoint her, but this was crazy.

It couldn't happen. It just couldn't.

Noel was Lil's best friend, and sex with him—even for the benefit of a baby for Lil—was creepy.

Okay. Not creepy.

And that was the problem.

Nila had loved Noel for a decade, but he was her sister's husband. And no one else knew that horrible secret. Not Lil. And certainly not Noel. There absolutely could not be anything physical between Nila and Noel, no matter what. Nila's heart couldn't take it.

She'd nursed that crush and suppressed it when Lil married him. Nila had gotten the next best thing—his friendship. And that was enough. It worked well for all of them. Sleeping with him would mess with the delineated boundaries of their relationship.

So, no way.

But Nila would have to be careful so not to upset Lil.

Nila cleared her throat. She refused to even acknowledge making love to Noel. "The thing is, Lil, Noel won't consider artificial insemination." She might be willing to give up nine months to house her niece or nephew, but she was not willing to go down the path of making love to Noel to do it.

"I know that. We're going to have to do it the old-fashioned way."

Nila shook her head in disbelief.

"Yes. Having sex." Lil raised her voice in defense.

"With Noel?" Nila cocked her head and stared hard into the face of her sister to make sure she had the facts straight. Lil couldn't really expect Nila to have sex with Noel or him to agree to it.

"Of course with Noel."

"Lil, the old-fashioned way would be to give up."

"Please."

"No!" Heat suffused through Nila. *Please don't tell me Noel is in on this. Was he actually contemplating...?*

"I will do anything."

"I am not sleeping with Noel." There had been a time long ago when she had been working up to it, having a relationship with Noel that was more than just a friendship. But then she had brought him home one Thanksgiving and caught him and Lil making out less than twenty-four hours later. Within six months, they were married with Nila as the maid of honor. Shortly thereafter, she transferred to the University of Tennessee and lived there after graduating until their mom became sick.

"It's the only way."

"It isn't the only way."

"He won't agree to artificial insemination."

"Because of me, Lil. I'm the problem." Noel might have said asking her to be a surrogate wouldn't be fair to her, but Nila knew the truth. He wanted Lil's baby, not Nila's.

"No, I'm the problem. You're the solution."

"Look. If Noel and I...have sex, I might...you know...start liking him. It could mess everything up. I don't want to be the other woman."

"I'd be honored for you to be the other woman."

"I can't have sex with him."

Lil heaved a sigh and stood. "I better go." She reached her hands out for Daisy.

Nila relinquished the kitten. "Don't leave mad."

"I'm not mad. I know I'm asking a lot, but it's the only way I can think of that won't take forever."

"A couple of years on the adoption list isn't forever."

Lil flinched as if Nila had hit her. "A couple of years is too long." She walked to the back door and opened it.

Nila followed her to the back porch. "You've been trying for seven. What's two more years?"

Lil didn't answer. She began to descend the wooden stairs but stopped short. "What's that?"

Nila looked beyond her sister to a stream of smoke from down the block. "It's probably just a barbecue or something."

"Somebody's...house...is on...fire."

Oh, boy. Lil is having an asthma attack. She'd had asthma since she'd been in a car fire that had claimed their father's life. She hated open fire of any kind—even going so far as replacing the gas stove with an electric range when she and Noel bought the house they lived in. She hadn't had an asthma attack brought on by seeing fire in years. Not since just before their Mom had died.

Lil gasped for breath. She staggered down the stairs and stood grasping the rail. Her labored breathing worsened.

"Just calm down. Calm down, Lil." Picking up her sister's purse, Nila wrenched it open and looked for her atomizer.

Where is it?

Nila turned the purse over and dumped it on the ground. Why'd she keep so much crap in her purse? Nila spotted the inhaler and picked it up, shaking it as she did so. She pulled off the cap and held it to Lil's mouth pressing down on the atomizer to deliver the medicine. Nila rubbed her back and peered into her face, making sure her twin was getting some relief.

"Okay?"

Lil nodded.

Nila then turned her attention to the smoke from down the block. "That smoke appears to be coming from the Jones' backyard. It's probably just the Jones boys playing with their dad's fire pit. Not worth getting upset over."

"They...shouldn't play...with fire."

Nila knelt down and gathered up the scattered contents on the ground and began putting them back in Lil's purse. "They're kids. That's what kids do. You better get used to it if you really want a baby. One day you'll come home and Junior's going to have a box of used matches and a guilty smile on his face." She stood and handed the purse and key ring to her sister. "You can't freak out on him like this."

Lil took the purse and walked around the corner of the house to the driveway where she'd parked her SUV. Lil pressed her key remote and the car chirped, its doors unlocking automatically. "Does this mean you're...going to do it?"

Nila sighed. "Has Noel actually agreed to this?"

"He will. He will...come around. He's always wanted...kids. He'll get used to the idea... He'll be so grateful to...hold his son, to have his son. You'll...see."

Nila reached forward to the bundle Lil still cradled to her chest. Scratching the kitten's ears, Nila refused to meet her twin's appealing gaze.

Noel won't agree. Oh, please, God, don't let him agree to do this.

Nila had to convince Noel to agree to the insemination. Otherwise....

Nila gulped. Oh, no. There absolutely could not be an otherwise.

****

They met on the court. Nila dribbled and threw a hook shot. Noel blocked, but he was too slow.

"Why won't you agree to artificial insemination?"

"I'm not talking with you any more about this." He caught the ball and threw it right back to the basket.

Nila jumped and blocked it, dribbling and pivoting out of his reach "Dearing, don't be such a jerk. You know how bad she wants a kid."

"It wasn't meant to be." He stole the ball and blocked her retrieval with his arm.

"I don't accept that."

"Well, you're both going to have to." He ran across the court, jumped, and shot. The ball arced through the air and scored without even touching the rim.

The ball bounced, and Nila palmed it. "You want kids." She dribbled, and Noel attempted a steal.

"But Lil can't have them."

"I can, and I'm willing." Nila blocked, faked a left, turned, and shot the ball. It ricocheted off the rim, and Noel caught it before it hit the ground.

"No."

She watched him pounding down the court, sweat making his shirt stick to his muscular back. She took off after him, reaching him before he could shoot. "Our genes are the same."

"No."

Nila raised her arms to block Noel's throw. "Are you afraid your kid will turn out like me instead of her?" For a second she took her eyes off the ball and focused on his face. She didn't want it to be, but his answer was important.

"There's nothing wrong with you." He didn't make eye contact, but used her brief distraction to shoot, and nailed the basket.

Except you chose her. The thought popped into her head, surprising her with the intensity of the feeling accompanying it.

Nila gave up the basketball game, resting her hands on her hips and attempting to sound convincing even though her lungs were burning from exertion. "Dearing, there's only one alternative, if you won't agree to doing it in a cup."

"That's bullshit!" Noel rested the ball under his arm and nailed her with a harsh look. "The only alternative is no kids." His response left no doubt in Nila's mind Lil had mentioned the sleeping with her to reproduce plan. Oh, but it hurt. To think sleeping with her repulsed him that much. It raised her hackles.

"She is about to lose a part of herself that makes her a woman. What if you had to have your testicles cut off? You think it wouldn't bother you?"

"Oh, spare me, Nila! This is none of your business, and you can butt the hell out of my marriage." He slammed the ball against the wall and stalked out of the gym.

Nila watched him leave. *No way. No how.*

He'd rather be childless than to suffer through sex with her.

Well? Did it entice you enough to read more?

If so, find it at your favorite online bookstore or in print at Amazon.

About Jennifer Johnson

Who am I?

I am a writer.

I write contemporary romantic fiction.

On some days, I aspire to be Wonder Woman wearing the awesome leotard and criminal fighting boots.

On other days, I am Wonder Woman with my Lasso of Truth and my no-nonsense pursuit of justice.

I live in the south across the river from the Midwest. I'm married to Super Man with a Tony Stark mind. We have Wonder/Super children, a bionic dog, and 3 mediocre cats. All in all, it's a comic book kind of life.

You can find out more about me at my website:
www.booksbyjenniferjohnson.com

and connect with me on Facebook at
https://facebook.com/booksbyjenniferjohnson

And through Twitter at
https://twitter.com/@BooksbyJennifer

JENNIFER JOHNSON BOOKS